18 MRCH.		

Please return this book on or before the date shown above. To renew go to www.essex.gov.uk/libraries, ring 0845 603 7628 or go to any Essex library.

DS12 4005

Essex County Council

GW00492732

For Tod Clark and Paul Legerski

*Two guys who know their way
around a whiskey glass...*

AUTHOR'S NOTE:

Blood and Whiskey is the second in a series of short novels I plan to produce roughly every two to three months. Each title will likely be between 50,000 and 60,000 words, though some may run slightly longer, depending on the needs of the story. The first in this series was 68 Kill, a book about which acclaimed author Brian Keene said, "68 Kill may very well be the perfect New Pulp novel." Each of these short novels will first be made available in inexpensive digital and paperback editions. However, I have also partnered with specialty book publisher Thunderstorm Books to produce collectible hardcover editions of each of these titles via my own imprint called Bitter Ale. For more information—and to sign up for Bitter Ale releases—visit the link below:

http://thunderstormbooks.com/thunderstorm/tsb_book/bryan-smiths-bitter-ale-series/

Blood and Whiskey

1

Johnny Doyle was on his third Maker's Mark double of the afternoon when Nora Lewis walked into The Delirium Lounge and sat next to him at the bar. Rather than immediately acknowledging her presence, Johnny tapped his cigarillo against the rim of the ashtray in front of him and kept his gaze on the television mounted behind the bar.

The Cubs were playing the Yankees at Wrigley Field in the top frame of an interleague doubleheader. The Cubbies were losing by half a dozen runs in the bottom of the third. Johnny liked baseball, but he'd stopped paying regular attention to standings and whatnot a long time ago. He couldn't get used to some of the weird ways the game had changed over the years. There were several teams with names he didn't recognize, for one thing, and he was never clear on whether they were entirely new teams or if they were old teams that had changed their names for inexplicable reasons. That was bad enough, but this interleague stuff was the worst. The goddamn Yankees shouldn't be playing at Wrigley Field in the middle of the summer. He was surprised people weren't rioting in the streets over this nonsense.

The bartender poured Nora a pint of porter and set the glass in front of her. Nora drained a third of it before finally addressing Johnny. "Your team winning, Johnny?"

Johnny blew a perfect smoke ring over the bar. This was a trick that had impressed the ladies more twenty years ago. A lot fewer of them smoked these days. He still wasn't looking at Nora. "I don't have a team."

"Have money riding on the outcome?"

"Nope."

"That's funny."

Johnny blew another smoke ring. "What do you mean?"

"For a guy with no team to pull for and no stake in how it turns out, you seem pretty fascinated with this game."

Johnny shrugged. "Something to do."

Nora drank more of her porter. "There are more interesting ways to pass the time. I could suggest a few."

Johnny wedged the cigarillo into one of the ashtray's rim notches and picked up the nearly empty glass of Maker's Mark. "I'm not really looking to get into anything too exciting these days. Not that I don't appreciate the concern."

Nora put a hand on his thigh. "You sure about that?"

Johnny drained the last of the Maker's Mark and pushed the glass across the bar. "I'm sure."

Nora took her hand away from his thigh and shrugged. "Your loss."

Johnny nodded. "I'm sure about that, too."

Nora shook her head. "Don't tell me you're still hung up on Lily."

She was talking about his wife of seven years, who'd left him just over a year ago. Lily was a tall brunette with the kind of build that guaranteed instant male attraction wherever she went. She had a face that combined angelic beauty with a generous hint of tempting wantonness.

Those first several years with Lily had been the best of his life. He had a good job and the woman of his dreams. But at some point his dream girl got restless and strayed from the marriage vows. It crushed him when he found out and he'd responded by behaving in some predictably pitiable ways. He even told her he knew how hard it must have been for her to resist temptation when she was constantly being pursued by practically every guy she met. He also told her he was willing to give her a second chance with no further recriminations. They would wipe the slate clean and go on from there. Lily laughed in his face and soon moved out of the house. Divorce papers were served shortly thereafter.

Just like that, it was over.

Seven years down the goddamn drain.

Johnny sipped from a fresh Maker's Mark. "I'm not still hung up on Lily."

Nora snorted. "Bullshit."

Johnny shrugged. "Believe what you want, Nora."

"I'll tell you what I believe."

"This should be good."

"I think you still can't accept what's happened." She glanced at the bartender, who was standing with his back to the bar and watching the game. She leaned a little closer to Johnny and dropped her voice some. "You're stuck in a rut because there's a part of you that thinks you can still win her back. Where Lily's concerned, you're not capable of being rational. You're in total denial. And it's pathetic, Johnny."

"If I'm so pathetic, why are you hitting on me?"

Nora chuckled and took another long drink from her glass of porter. "Just trying to do my good deed for the day. What you need is distraction. I think I could fuck Lily out of your head if you'd let me. God knows *somebody* needs to do it."

Johnny looked at Nora, giving her his full attention for the first time. She was no Lily, but women of that caliber were a rare breed. It still boggled his mind that he'd ever managed to hook up with Lily in the first place. It was a case of all the stars aligning in just the right way at the right time. Somehow he'd impressed a goddess enough to make her want to marry him. He knew the odds of ever making another goddess fall in love with him were low.

Nora was a sexy girl in her own right, just in a more earthbound kind of way. She was slender and had shoulder-length ash-blonde hair in a stylish cut. Today she was wearing three-inch black heels, stockings, and a sleek strapless dress.

Nora always looked well-put-together, but perhaps a little more so than usual today. Johnny was pretty sure he knew why.

He had been out of work for going on two months. It was no big deal. He'd done well over the years and had a decent amount of money socked away. Theoretically he could go another couple years before things started getting tight, barring any kind of unforeseen catastrophe, of course. It all meant he was in no big hurry to dive back into the workforce.

It also meant his day-to-day routine had congealed into predictable patterns. Nora running into him here was no accident. She knew he had become an afternoon regular at The Delirium Lounge and had come looking for him. And she'd done so with one overriding purpose in mind.

To fuck Lily out of my head.

She smiled as she watched him check her out. He had to reluctantly admit bedding Nora might not be the worst idea in the world. She was right, of course. Lily was never coming back, regardless of how desperately he continued to pine for her. It might do him a world of good to lie down with a woman again, even if she wasn't the one he really wanted. He felt a strong surge of desire at just having entertained the thought. He hadn't been physically intimate with anyone since getting dumped by Lily. A year was a long damn time to go without sex.

Nora was right.

It could be the start of getting his head on straight again. He was about to make a grudging admission along those lines when she said something that killed the words before he could speak them.

"Speaking of Lily, I saw her hanging out with Slick today."

Johnny frowned. "With Slick Hogan? Are you sure?"

Nora rolled her eyes. "Do you know any other Slick? Yes, Johnny, I'm sure."

Johnny scratched his chin. "Huh."

Slick Hogan was an obnoxious twenty-something guy who spent much of his time hanging out on the square, though it struck Johnny now that he hadn't seen the son of a bitch in a while. He was white as snow, but he dressed and talked like he was from the hood. The gangsta wannabe shtick was a harmless enough affectation, but Slick was widely reputed to be a drug dealer. And not a weed dealer, either. Slick was said to move harder stuff, primarily cocaine.

Nora finished her porter and nodded for a refill when the bartender looked her way. "I know, right? I was shocked, too."

Johnny laughed. "You mean he was chatting her up on the square, right? Slick flirts with all the pretty town ladies who cross his path."

Nora shook her head. "That's not what I mean. I saw them in line together at Kroger. And they were definitely *together*, if you get my drift. They were buying cheap beer and she was hanging on to him. She looked rough, like she might fall over if she let go of him. To tell you the truth, she looked sort of strung out."

Johnny started getting angry as he listened to her. "You're full of shit, Nora. You're just running Lily down because you want to get with me."

The look she gave him was full of pity. "I'm not making any of this up, swear to God. Shit, you can find out for yourself easily enough."

Johnny gave her a long, measuring look and decided she was being honest. His reflexive denial couldn't obscure the truth of what he felt in his bones.

Lily was in trouble.

Shit.

He stubbed out his cigarillo and threw back his fourth Maker's Mark double in a single big gulp. He put the empty glass on the bar, slid off his stool, and dug out his wallet.

Nora frowned. "What are you doing, Johnny?"

Johnny threw some bills down on the bar and looked at her. "I'm sorry, but I've gotta run. I'll check in with you later."

He walked out of The Delirium Lounge before she could say anything else.

2

Johnny considered hailing a cab for the ride across town to Lily's place. Four double whiskeys was probably more than enough to raise his blood alcohol level a bit above the legal limit, but no cabs were waiting at the curb outside, which caused him to debate whether to take the chance and drive. In truth, he frequently drove after drinking too much. On the other hand, he was rarely ever as agitated as he felt now. He was worried his mental state and buzz would add up to a dangerous combination.

His Austin-Healey convertible was parked in one of the angled slots at the curb outside the Delirium Lounge. He weighed the decision as he stood next to the vintage car, the rational part of his brain telling him he was overreacting to Nora's news. There was no good reason to rush. He could spare the few minutes it would take for a cab to swing by. It rarely took longer than that for one to circle around to this stretch of the square, a shopping and dining area that was one of the more interesting places to hang out in the little college city of Murfreesboro. It was where Johnny spent most of his time these days.

A police cruiser pulled into an angled slot next to the Austin-Healey. Moments later the cop driving it got out and shot a grin at Johnny. "What's up, Doyle? Not thinking about driving under the influence, are you?"

"Just getting some fresh air, Joe."

"That why you got your keys out, bud?"

Joe Voss was one of Johnny's old high school buddies. The guy was still one of his closest male friends. There was little real chance he would bust his him for impaired driving. Still, it would probably be best to err on the side of caution.

He shoved the keys into his hip pocket. "Was just getting my Zippo. Forgot I'd left the damn thing in the car."

Joe frowned. "Uh-huh. Where's the Zippo now?"

Johnny patted his shirt's breast pocket. "Right here."

Joe nodded. "Right. Well, you just be careful, you hear? Call me this weekend and we'll grab a brew."

"Sure, sounds good."

Joe Voss got back in his cruiser, backed out of the angled slot, and drove away. Within moments, a yellow cab came down the street and turned left in front of the Delirium Lounge. Johnny stepped into the street and signaled the driver with a raised arm.

The cab stopped.

Johnny slid into the back and gave the driver an address.

3

The cab dropped him off at the corner of Duvall Street. Johnny paid the fare and over-tipped the driver. The cabbie's eyes widened when he waved off the change. This was another habit Johnny had developed in the post-Lily phase of his life. He had always been more generous than the norm when it came to compensating service people, but these days it went beyond a standard level of generosity. He so rarely felt good about anything lately and throwing some money around where he could was an easy way to counteract that.

He dug the Zippo and a cigarillo from his breast pocket and lit up as he started down the street. The neighborhood where Lily lived now wasn't exactly the ghetto, but it was significantly less upscale than the one where she and Johnny had shared a home for the better part of a decade, a house that was in his name and predated the marriage. Still, he'd been surprised by her failure to attempt a claim on it in the divorce. Hell, she hadn't contested much of anything. She did it because she wanted a quick, clean break. She wanted Johnny Doyle out of her life as soon as possible and she didn't care what she had to give up to make that happen.

Johnny still couldn't figure that out.

He wasn't a bad guy.

He didn't smell funny.

So what the hell?

Several of the houses on Duvall Street had front yards surrounded by chain-link fences. A few windows here and there were covered by iron bars. Even so, there was no real sense of danger. This was a safe place to go strolling alone, at least in broad daylight. Not that he had far to walk. Lily shared a duplex with a roommate a couple blocks down the street. Johnny could have had the cabbie drop him right outside her door, but he'd wanted to get the lay of the land first. Nora's tale had stirred a host of concerns, one of the big ones being her environment and who she was surrounding herself with these days. He still couldn't credit the implication that she'd fallen into some kind of drugged-out relationship with Slick Hogan. Lily was better than that. And, he liked to think, smarter than that.

Maybe Nora had misinterpreted some things.

He could hope so, anyway.

There was no chain-link fence around the yard in front of Lily's duplex. The yard was well-kept and there were no bars on the windows. It didn't look so bad, really, even if Johnny couldn't picture living here himself. Lily had cut off all contact with him once the divorce was final and had never shared her new address with him. Johnny, though, had looked it up on the Internet. Goddamn useful tool, the Internet. It sure made stalking a hell of a lot easier than it had been back in the day.

Lily's silver Honda Civic was parked in the driveway by the side of her half of the duplex. Her ride was another significant step down from her time with him. She'd sold her Lexus and acquired the 80's-era Civic on the cheap. This was another thing Johnny had discovered via the magic of the Internet. He was friends with her on Facebook and she had talked about it there.

She didn't know they were Facebook friends. On Facebook, Johnny was "Joanna Walker", a person who didn't actually exist. He didn't interact with her much out of fear of giving himself away, but it was a good way to keep tabs on her. But he would have guessed the Honda was hers even without the aid of that questionable bit of subterfuge. The array of stickers on the back supporting crackpot political causes and advertising bands hardly anyone had ever heard of was a dead giveaway.

Johnny stood at the end of the driveway and smoked half his cigarillo while he worked up the guts to walk up there and ring the doorbell. She wouldn't be happy to see him, no question about that. She would probably scream or threaten to call the police. Lily hadn't been a temperamental type while they were married, but he doubted she would react positively to his unannounced—and unwelcome—appearance at her doorstep.

Johnny sighed.

Fuck it.

He dropped the cigarillo on the driveway and crushed it out beneath the heel of his boot. After taking a final moment to steel his nerves, he started up the driveway.

4

The doorbell was dead. Johnny deduced this by the way no sound was produced after he'd repeatedly pushed the button. This brilliant insight made him wonder whether he ought to consider a career change. Clearly he had missed his true calling by not going into the field of private detecting.

Johnny rapped his knuckles against the door a few times, hard enough that anyone awake inside should have heard it. He moved back a step to await the appearance of either Lily or her roommate, an attractive if sort of trampy-looking blonde named Bree. Joanna Walker was also friends with Bree on Facebook. It still struck him as odd that people were so willing to accept strangers as "friends" on social media sites. Then again, whenever he mentioned this to anyone, he was accused of being an out-of-touch curmudgeon. Maybe it was so.

Johnny glanced at his TAG Heuer watch.

More than a full minute had passed since he'd knocked. There was no sound of movement from the other side of the door, nor did he detect any hushed voices whispering to each other. There was a possibility Lily had seen him coming up the driveway and had decided to pretend she wasn't home. It would be in keeping with her program of total avoidance, though he liked to imagine she wasn't rude enough not to at least open the door and tell him to get lost face-to-face.

More minutes passed.

Johnny knocked on the door again, harder this time, with the base of his fist. The door rattled in its frame. He regretted this almost immediately. A nosy neighbor might think he was being belligerent or that some kind of domestic incident was in progress, one that might require a call to 911. The latter was a ridiculous notion, but Johnny had learned long ago not to underestimate the tendency of people to overreact and do stupid shit, his very presence on this doorstep being a classic case in point.

No one came to the door. He resisted the urge to knock yet again, ditto the alternative impulse to alert anyone inside to his presence by shouting. It was probably time to give up. He should just dig out his cell phone and summon another cab to take him back to the Delirium Lounge. Nora might still be there. Maybe they could hook up, after all.

Yeah, that would undoubtedly be the smart way to go.

Johnny stepped off the porch and stared at the first-floor windows. Closed wooden shutters obscured any possible view of the interior. After a quick glance around to verify he wasn't being watched, Johnny moved to the side of the building, where there was just one window on the bottom floor. He couldn't see in through there, either. This was getting to be a little aggravating. After another look out at the street and around at the neighboring houses, Johnny decided to risk venturing around to the back of the house and started in that direction.

He knew this wasn't what anyone would describe as an advisable course of action. By going around to the back he was coming perilously close to trespassing. If someone called the cops and he was caught poking around in his ex-wife's back yard, it could potentially result in some embarrassing consequences. Lily would probably take out a restraining order against him and word would get out that he'd been caught stalking her. God help him if it somehow led to him being unmasked as Joanna Walker. He'd never live that shit down. If there was even the smallest chance Lily was in some kind of real trouble, however, he had to at least try to ascertain the extent of the problem, even if most people would say her well-being was no longer any of his damn business.

A window at the back of the duplex wasn't shuttered and afforded him a view of an empty kitchen. He could also see down a short hallway that presumably led to the living room. It, too, was empty. A few things concerned him. For one, the kitchen was a mess. There were empty beer and liquor bottles on every surface. The beer was the "cheap" kind Nora had claimed she'd spotted Lily buying earlier in the day, which lent her story a new level of credence. Also, there was a pile of dirty dishes in the sink, as well as several inches of rancid-looking standing water. This evidence of domestic squalor was bad enough—he'd always known Lily to keep a neat and clean household—but the thing that bothered him most was the back door. It was standing open. Not by much, no more than a half inch, but open it undeniably was.

Johnny weighed his next move. The door being open didn't necessarily mean anything bad had occurred here. Maybe Lily or Bree had left it ajar by mistake after taking out the trash. Or they had been partying too hard and merely neglected to shut it all the way after returning from a beer run. There were a million possible mundane explanations.

But Johnny didn't like it.

Nor did he like Lily's failure to come to the door despite the presence of her car in the driveway. Again, this wasn't necessarily a legitimate cause for concern. Nor, really, was anything in the messy kitchen. There were no visible indications of foul play, nothing that showed evidence of a struggle. His common sense told him the obvious—Lily had just become a careless drunk. She was probably passed out upstairs after one too many cheap beers. There was just one sensible thing to do here—call that cab and walk away, having learned a valuable lesson about minding his own business. If his paranoia about her situation persisted, he could go to a pay phone and call in an anonymous tip, have the police come check the place out.

Yep.

That was absolutely what he should do.

Johnny nudged the back door open a little wider with the toe of his boot and poked his head inside. "Anyone in here? Lily, are you home? It's, um, me, Johnny."

It felt like a really wise idea to identify himself. Lily would recognize his voice immediately, but Bree would not. He didn't want the girl to open up on him with her .357 Magnum. She had posted pictures of herself posing with it on Facebook. The most striking one had shown her sighting down the weapon's long barrel with a sexy leer on her face. She looked like the kind of girl who wouldn't hesitate to bust a cap in an intruder's ass. And getting shot with a high-caliber handgun was near the top of Johnny's list of things he'd prefer to never experience if at all possible.

No one responded to his entreaties. Johnny nudged the door open a little farther and stepped into the kitchen, telling himself it didn't count as breaking and entering if someone had left the door open. He was just a concerned citizen doing his civic duty. This was maybe stretching the truth dangerously thin, but he didn't care. He was now a prisoner of his paranoia and had no choice but to see this foolish escapade through to the end.

Johnny paused by the dining table as he moved deeper into the little kitchen. Its surface was littered with typical party debris—empty bottles and cans, overflowing ashtrays, and a paper plate with a partially-devoured roast beef and Cheetos sandwich. There was a residue of what looked like cocaine near the edge of the table. He dipped a fingertip in the residue, put it to a nostril, and sniffed.

Yep. That is definitely cocaine.

It was yet another damning detail backing up Nora's account of Lily's drugged-out demeanor at the grocery store. Johnny just didn't get it. Sure, he'd known her to smoke a little weed now and then, but he never would have imagined her getting hooked up with cokeheads. When he caught up to Lily, he meant to have a serious conversation with her whether she wanted his input or not. He likely couldn't do jack shit to help her, but it behooved him to at least *try*.

Shit, he loved her.

And he was *definitely* still hung up on her, despite what he'd told Nora.

He entered the short hallway beyond the kitchen and approached the living room. "Is anybody home? This is Johnny Doyle, Lily's ex-husband. I heard something today that made me worry and I just want to check on her. I'm not here to cause trouble or rob the place, so please don't fucking shoot me. Okay?"

Nothing.

The living room was empty.

Johnny again felt vaguely ridiculous talking to himself. Like the kitchen, the living room was a disaster area. Bottles and cans were everywhere. An empty pizza box sat on the floor in front of the television. Pizza crumbs were on the carpet. The drugs and the mess made him wonder whether Lily might be overcompensating for getting married too young at twenty-six. She was in her mid-thirties now so overdoing the wild and reckless thing in a desperate attempt to recapture something that was lost certainly fit the vibe of what he was seeing here.

He announced himself one last time as he started up the staircase to the second floor. "Anybody up here? Don't shoot. I just need to check on Lily."

No answer.

There were two bedrooms and a hallway bathroom upstairs. The bathroom was empty, as was the first bedroom he checked, which was predictably a wreck and redolent with the faintly musky odor of recent sex. A giant red dildo and handcuffs rested atop a black nightstand. He spotted another cocaine residue next to the dildo.

He moved on to the second bedroom.

Which was not empty.

5

There was a dead woman on the bed. That she was dead and not merely asleep was obvious for a number of reasons. She had long dark hair like Lily's, as well as a similar build, but immediate identification of the deceased wasn't possible. Someone had beaten her face into an unrecognizable pulp with a hammer. The hammer was next to the corpse on the blood-spattered mattress.

Johnny's heart almost seized up at the sight of the bloody tableau. He had expected only to discover more evidence of a sadly drug-infested lifestyle. Despite the open back door, there had never been serious expectation of stumbling upon the scene of a vicious crime. The possibility that the dead woman was Lily made him want to scream. She had treated him with great callousness toward the end of their marriage, yes, but that didn't matter now. For the first several moments following the discovery, the world felt like it was spinning around him and he had to lean against the doorjamb to keep from falling over. A nearly overpowering repulsion at the sight of the ravaged corpse almost sent him running out of the house.

But he couldn't leave without at least attempting a closer examination of the body. He needed to be totally sure it was really her before deciding whether to notify the police via anonymous tip or pursue some other course, such as exacting vengeance on Lily's behalf. That the latter scenario was fool-hardy and ill-advised at best—and potentially suicidal at worst—was beyond doubt. Letting the authorities handle the matter was

17

the wise way to go, but if this really was Lily, odds were he wouldn't be capable of rational thoughts or deeds for some time to come.

He pushed away from the doorframe and moved a few steps deeper into the room. Blood was seemingly everywhere he looked—on the carpeted floor, on the nightstand, and on the wall behind the headboard. He pictured the killer working frenziedly, grunting as the hammer went rapidly up and down, smashing flesh and pulverizing teeth and cheekbones. Flecks of curdling pink tissue clinging to it indicated the claw end had been used, too. The revelation made Johnny shake his head in dismay even as it further inflamed his rage. Surely only a true psychopath could do something so brutal.

There were tattoos on the woman's arms. One image was of a colorful sugar skull. A larger one depicted the face of a wolf against a night sky with a full moon in the background. She had one more little tattoo near her pierced navel—a green four-leaf clover. Lily had been tattoo-free prior to leaving him. He tried to take some comfort in this knowledge, but he knew the skin illustrations didn't necessarily mean the dead woman wasn't Lily. Getting some ink would be another thing that jibed with what he knew of her post-divorce behavior pattern.

He steeled his nerves again and got right up to the edge of the bed. Upon closer inspection, the dead woman's build was distressingly similar to Lily's, but he thought maybe the breasts were a little smaller. Whether this was an accurate impression or just a hopeful illusion made possible by the way a woman's breasts will spread out some in the prone position, he did not know. Otherwise, however, the proportions were very, very close to what he remembered. The height was right, too. It was probably her. He was almost ninety-percent certain at this point. But still…there was that little smidgen of doubt. More than a year had passed since he'd last been this close to Lily. His memory regarding all the little contours of her body might be just a little off.

Johnny grimaced and felt his stomach flutter when he realized there was only one way he could be absolutely sure the dead woman was her.

No, he thought. *I don't want to do that. I can't.*

His head began to hurt. Too much time had elapsed since his last whiskey. It was the premature onset of hangover symptoms familiar to those with a relationship with booze that went beyond the casual. One or two drinks and he would have been fine. But four Maker's Mark doubles in the afternoon meant he'd been on his way to getting good and plastered. Cutting an incipient bender off midstream was never a good idea, at least for the alcoholically inclined. It always resulted in symptoms like these and being in the presence of a badly mutilated corpse was making it a thousand times worse. He felt woozy and sweaty and needed another drink to get back on an even keel. There had to be a bottle of hooch around here Lily's cretinous friends hadn't already consumed.

But he didn't have time to go searching for one and knew it. He had to make the positive identification and get one with figuring out his next step.

He gritted his teeth and bent closer to Lily.

Shit, he thought. *I really, really, really* don't *want to do this.*

Lily had a small, distinctive birth mark on her lower back that resembled the shape of a bird in flight. He needed to roll the body over and check for the birthmark. Handling the bloody corpse of a murder victim would be unpleasant—to say the least—but it was the only way to be certain the dead woman was Lily.

A few things struck him as he bent even closer to the corpse. This woman had been killed very recently. The blood was still wet. Also, the flesh was still warm. Johnny thought about the open back door. Perhaps the killer had gone out that way. It made sense. Unless he'd taken the time to clean himself up, he would have been a blood-covered mess. In that case, it'd be better to go out the back way. It would mean less chance of being spotted by a neighbor.

Johnny had just slid a hand beneath one of the woman's shoulders when he heard the rattle of a key in the front door lock downstairs. A moment later, the door creaked open and he heard voices, male and female.

Seconds later, he heard footsteps coming up the stairs.

6

He was hiding inside the closet by the time the man and woman entered the bedroom. The closet was one of those long, narrow ones with accordion-style doors. The doors had narrow, shutter-like slats through which it was possible to catch a fractured glimpse of what was happening in the room. The slats were angled downward, which meant it would be difficult for anyone in the room to see inside the closet, but knowing that didn't make Johnny feel any safer.

His heart was pounding and he was working hard to keep his breath from coming out in harsh, painfully audible little gasps. The urge to retreat to a far end of the closet and do his best to hide behind some of the hanging garments was strong. That he was in a woman's closet was clear from the array of dangling dresses, blouses, and stylish jackets. Movement, however, was complicated by the many pairs of shoes on the closet's floor. There were boots, sneakers, pumps, and slutty heels of varying come-fuck-me proportions. It was too easy to imagine stumbling over them en route to the end of the closet, so Johnny made himself stay where he was for the time being, though retreat remained an option should one of the killers make a move toward the closet.

And that was another thing. Whatever had happened to the woman on the bed, there was more than one guilty party. Probably only one of them had pounded on her face with the hammer, but that made the other person no less complicit based on what he'd heard so far.

"All right," a woman's voice said, "so how are we gonna do this?"

He didn't recognize the voice, though it had a distinctively deep, sultry quality to it. It was the kind of voice that immediately made any woman much more alluring to him, but not this time. Because the hard reality here was he was in mortal danger. These people were murderers and he was an after-the-fact witness to the gruesome evidence of their crime. If they discovered his presence, they wouldn't hesitate to kill him.

And Johnny Doyle had no desire to die.

Not on this day or any other.

For one thing, becoming dead would complicate his ability to catch a decent buzz on occasion. Getting killed would also squash any possibility of avenging Lily's probable death. These things were major potential bummers for sure, but mostly he didn't want to die because being alive was obviously better in every possible way. Wanting to keep on living no matter what was the most basic human instinct of all and right now Johnny was feeling the truth of that more starkly than he ever had before.

A male voice said, "I think we need to, like, *dismember* the bitch. It'd make her easier to carry for one thing. And we could, you know, maybe get rid of different pieces of her in a bunch of different places."

The woman snorted. "Why in fuck would we do that? It's too complicated. And it would increase the risk of getting caught because you'd be spending all that extra fucking time carrying around pieces of the body."

The guy said, "But it'd make her a lot harder to identify. That'd be good, right?"

This was Slick Hogan talking. Johnny hadn't talked to the dope-slinging jackass in a while, but he remembered the voice well. Slick seemed to have ditched the faux-gangsta patois, though. The woman he couldn't be a hundred percent sure about, but he figured she was probably Bree Sloan, Joanna Walker's gun-toting Facebook pal.

The woman sighed. "It might make immediate identification harder, but an eventual DNA identification would still be possible. The best thing would be to destroy the body completely. I mean every last fucking *trace*. Make it like she never goddamn existed in the first place."

"How would we do that?"

Johnny bit back a gasp as he detected movement in the room. One of the killers came abruptly closer to the closet, their form momentarily blotting out much of his already obstructed view of the room. He stifled a relieved sigh when whoever it was moved away just as abruptly. Fighting his nerves, he put his face closer to the door slats for a better view. The woman was the person moving around. He saw right away she was indeed Bree Sloan. She was even better-looking in person. The trampy quality conveyed by the low-res pictures on Facebook gave way in real life to a raw sexuality that would have been breathtaking under other, less horrendous circumstances.

Bree had a trim but curvy body and was wearing jeans so tight they looked painted on her skin. Black sunglasses were hooked over the V-neck collar of a fitted blue shirt. She was visibly more agitated than Slick and was pacing back and forth across the room, keeping her gaze riveted to the dead woman the whole time. "Maybe we could dissolve her body in lye. I've seen that done on TV shows."

Slick nodded. "Yeah, like on *Breaking Bad*. But the guy on that show's a fucking scientist or something. What if we don't do it right, use enough lye, or whatever? Where would we even get the lye? Fucking Wal-Mart?"

Bree stopped pacing and stood at the foot of the bed, facing the dead woman. "I guess we could Google it, but you're right, it would be too complicated. I wouldn't want to waste all that time and effort only to fuck it all up."

"Well, shit. Do you have any other ideas?"

Bree glanced at him. "No. Goddammit."

Johnny noted with mild curiosity that Slick had done more than just drop the stilted hip hop patter—he'd changed his entire image, appearing to have gone rockabilly. He'd grown his blond hair out and was wearing it in a slicked-back pompadour. He wore jeans with rolled-up cuffs, black engineer boots, and a bowling league shirt. The look was as contrived as his apparently now mothballed white rapper persona, but Johnny had to admit—grudgingly—that it actually suited him a good bit better. Though it pained him to think about it, he could now *almost* get why Lily might have become interested in him.

Bree shook her head. "I guess we just do this the old-fashioned way—roll her up in a sheet, stuff her in the trunk of your car, and bury her deep somewhere way out in the country. But we're also gonna have to clean the shit out of this place. We should get rid of all these sheets and the mattress cover, too. Maybe burn them up with her body before we pile the dirt over her."

Slick said, "Why the trunk of *my* car?"

"Because I said so."

Slick grunted. "That's some bullshit right there. We used my car last time. It's only fair you take some of the risk once in a while."

Johnny's breath caught in his throat.

So Lily's roommates were not first time killers. It made him wonder whether Lily had been a party to any previous violent crimes, perhaps after being coerced to go along with it by her sleazy new friends. Though he didn't much care for the idea, it would at least partly explain the drug use. She might have been numbing herself against the grim reality that had overtaken her life. And maybe these lunatics had killed her because she finally couldn't take it anymore. The bottom line was it was up to him to make sure something was done about it. He had to call the cops the moment he was able to get clear of this place. It would mean abandoning his fuzzily-conceived notions of personal vengeance, but that was probably for the best anyway. He had no experience with this kind of thing and in a confrontation he'd be as apt to get himself killed as avenge Lily's death. But getting out of here alive was going to be an easier said than done proposition. Though it was frustrating as hell, the best he could do at the moment was hang tight and wait for the opportunity that would hopefully be coming along soon.

But then an alternative idea occurred to him. He could dial 911 on his cell phone. The touchscreen was set to silent, which meant no annoying tapping sounds were produced when the buttons were used. He wouldn't be able to say anything, but he could let the operator listen to what was happening. They had to respond to every call no matter what. It was the law. He frowned as he thought about that. Was it really the law or was it a false impression he'd picked up somewhere?

He didn't know.

But it felt like his best option anyway.

So he reached into his hip pocket and began to carefully pull out his cell phone, making a mental note to turn down the volume control before placing the call. It wouldn't do to have the 911 operator's voice blaring out at the killers from the closet.

The phone came free of his pocket and he pulled up his contacts list, doing his best to ignore the increasingly angry sounds of the argument transpiring in the bedroom. They were still going round and round about whose car they would use for body disposal. The longer they took working out the details, the greater the chances of the police getting here and catching them red-handed.

He had his thumb poised above the button for 911 when the gunshot rang out.

7

The sound of the gunshot was followed by a loud thump. Johnny figured this was a body hitting the floor. One of the killers had produced a gun from somewhere and shot the other one. He hadn't noticed a gun on either of them but there was no other explanation. Because his attention had been focused on his phone, he had no idea who had shot whom.

The unexpected report of the gun was so jarring it shocked him into dropping the phone. He also jumped back a little, knocking the back of his head on the rod from which Lily's wardrobe hung. The blow to the head didn't hurt too much, but it did squeeze a pained little gasp from him. Luckily the gunshot covered the noise. Regardless, he now endeavored to remain as still and silent as possible.

Johnny knew the killer couldn't hear his pounding heart, but to his own ears it seemed rock concert loud. A big part of him wanted to whimper like a timid forest animal cornered by much larger prey. Not doing so required a monumental effort of will. A few moments passed and the ringing in his ears began to fade a little. He heard a sigh from the bedroom and what sounded like someone kicking the corpse of the newly deceased.

"I guess that settles that, dumbass. We'll be using your fucking car for body disposal." The sound of yet another kick followed these words. "You know better than to argue with me, you stupid shit!"

And then there was still more kicking.

The speaker was Bree.

Some reflexive, helplessly perverse piece of his psyche
was relieved to hear her voice. It was the same lizard-brain response that made many men feel at least a flicker of desire for
any demonstrably evil but attractive woman. He'd felt it before
while watching news stories about women involved in notorious
murder cases. It meant nothing.

A low whimper emanated from the room. "I'm sorry.
Jesus. Please stop. "

Slick.

So he wasn't dead after all.

The revelation rendered Johnny almost dizzy with relief.
Slick was a no good piece of shit, but the relief was instinctive,
issuing from another base section of his psyche, the one from
which stemmed an aversion to being present at the scene of a
violent death—even if the no good piece of shit getting killed
deserved it.

Only now he knew it hadn't happened at all.

But that left some disturbing questions about what had
actually transpired. Though he hadn't seen it happen, his mind
quickly filled in the blanks in a way that felt so accurate it was
almost as if he *had* seen it go down. This Bree person was a
volatile, deeply unhinged personality. The gun had been stashed
away somewhere. Maybe in a drawer in the nightstand or under
the bed, who knew? But it'd been in the room somewhere. And
Bree had gotten so angry at Slick for arguing with her that she
had taken it from its hiding place and fired a warning shot.
Johnny's imagination supplied a vivid picture of Slick cringing
and then falling to the floor as the slug missed him by inches.

"Get up off your scrawny ass."

Johnny heard Slick grunt as he got to his feet. "Look,
have it your way. I don't care. But you shouldn't have done
that. What if a neighbor heard and called 911?"

"Then I guess we're fucked."

"You shouldn't fly off the handle like that. What's your
real problem, anyway?"

Bree sighed. "I'm just stressed the fuck out. I need more goddamn cocaine."

"So call Echo. She's got the hookup. Or Dez."

Bree groaned. "No way. I owe those crazy bitches too much money."

Slick laughed mirthlessly. "Money wouldn't be an issue if *someone* hadn't lost their shit and offed this bitch."

"You may be right, but there's no use crying over it now. Either the cops will come or they won't. For now, let's pretend all is cool and get down to business. Okay?"

Slick grumbled half-heartedly but soon bowed to Bree's pragmatic fatalism. She was right, of course. The cops would either come or they wouldn't. If they didn't show up, they still had a body to bury. But if the cops did come, the whole thing would be out of their hands and that would almost come as a relief. Neither verbalized this latter bit, but Johnny read it between the lines easily enough. The one thing he was a little confused about was the implication that a Lily who was still alive and breathing would have meant more money for them. Lily's days of being flush with cash had been over even before her death.

On the other hand, her roommates would have been well aware of her former living situation. Johnny was no Warren Buffett by any means, but he was filthy rich compared to these people. Maybe they'd been planning to use Lily to wrangle money out of him. The idea made some sense, but it meant Lily's murder was even more of a puzzle. They certainly wouldn't be getting any money from him now.

Sounds of work came from the bedroom as Johnny continued the struggle to remain absolutely silent. There was a rustling of cloth as they swept the comforter off the bed and untucked the sheet beneath Lily from the mattress. This was followed by a significant amount of grunting. Johnny figured they had twisted up the ends of the sheet and then used it as an improvised transfer sling to move the body to the floor.

He prayed they would go about their work quickly now that they'd settled their argument and get gone soon. His head was throbbing from the knock it'd taken and his back was getting stiff from remaining in the awkward position against the wall too long. He had his butt braced against the wall and the back of his head was wedged beneath the rod. One leg was locked beneath him, the sole of his shoe pressed solidly against the floor, but his other foot rested atop a pile of lady shoes. He was terrified his body would betray him as it became unable to maintain the position any longer. His mind taunted him with images of him tumbling out of the closet and landing at the feet of the astonished murderers.

After a time the sounds of work in the bedroom ceased and he heard Slick say, "All right, what now?"

"Go pull that crappy Nova of yours around to the back and get the trunk open. Make sure there's enough room for the all the crap we gotta haul away with us."

Johnny's rage rekindled upon hearing this.

Lily's body was part of the "crap" Bree was talking about. Hearing her referred to that way, as if she were nothing more than just another load of trash to be carried out, almost made him burst out of the closet and take a run at the murdering assholes, maybe see if he could get to that gun and blow them both away. It was a pure Hollywood fantasy notion with little to no chance of success, but for one galvanizing moment he stood on the edge of doing it anyway.

And then that moment passed.

Johnny Doyle was no Hollywood action hero.

"On it," Slick said. "Be right back."

"Hold on."

Slick made an exasperated sound. "What now?"

"Grab some trash bags from the kitchen. Some of the big black ones under the sink. There's some duct tape in a drawer. Get that, too."

"Why?"

Now it was Bree's turn to sound exasperated. "Because it's bad enough we're gonna be hauling all this bloody shit out of here in broad daylight. We'll wrap her up in the bags and bag up some of this other shit, too. Now get going, goddammit."

Slick grumbled a bit more, but soon departed to presumably do as he'd been told.

One of them being gone presented Johnny with a new dilemma. Maybe he should rush out and overwhelm Bree while she was alone. He would have the element of surprise on his side and might be able to pull it off. He could knock her down and get the gun before she had a chance to react. Then he could wait for Slick to return and...

He frowned.

And then what?

His frown deepened.

Kill them. That's what.

Johnny tried very hard to picture himself gunning down two human beings. It wasn't easy to picture, no matter how much they deserved it.

He stayed where he was.

Slick returned maybe five minutes later and they resumed their work. The process seemed to go on forever as Johnny's discomfort continued to worsen. At last, however, Bree pronounced the work done and there was some more grunting as they hauled Lily's body out of the bedroom. The room was then empty for a relatively lengthy period of time, long enough for Johnny to wonder whether it was time to emerge from his hiding place. They might already be en route to Lily's intended remote burial site, which meant it was high time he start taking some action, starting with calling 911. He couldn't give the operator a tag number, but he could provide a vivid description of the suspects, as well as what kind of car they would be driving.

Johnny stooped to retrieve his phone.

He had a hand on the closet door and was about to push it open when he heard footsteps come pounding up the stairs again. His heart lurched and his breath caught in his throat as the footsteps came running into the bedroom. He heard a sound of crinkling plastic seconds later and realized one of them had re-turned to fetch the rest of the bagged-up bloody evidence. Then whoever it was went running back out of the bedroom.

Johnny let out a breath.

His heart was hammering harder and faster than ever. One more moment and he would have been standing in the bed-room—or out in the hallway—as one of the killers returned. And that would have been that. The naked terror caused by the close call intensified the ache in his head by a magnitude of about a trillion.

He stood there another ten minutes.

And then another ten, long past the point where he thought they might return yet again.

At long last, he opened the closet door and stepped into the bedroom.

8

The bed had been thoroughly stripped. The comforter, the sheets, and the mattress cover were all gone. There was some staining on the mattress itself, but it wasn't dramatic-looking. A new mattress cover and sheets would obscure it easily enough, but the stain would nonetheless provide damning DNA evidence of the crime should an investigation ever uncover it. Replacing it was probably on their to-do list after they took care of the more immediate problem of corpse disposal. Same thing went for scrubbing the blood spatter from the headboard and the wall behind the bed.

Johnny's instincts screamed at him to immediately flee the place while he had the chance, but he opted to first document the remaining evidence with his cell phone's camera. He snapped a wide shot of the bed and the wall and then zoomed in for close-ups of both. He was on the verge of putting the phone away when he noted the hole in the wall above the nightstand lamp. The hole marked the path of the bullet fired by Bree during her moment of rage. For the first time it struck him how lucky he was that she hadn't fired the gun at the closet.

He took a picture of the hole and walked out of the room.

He moved hurriedly to the top of the staircase, took two steps down, and paused, his ears perking as he detected a low and barely audible sound. It took him a few moments to recognize it as the sound of someone breathing deeply in and out in their sleep.

Shit.

His first thought was that either Bree or Slick had stayed behind to take a nap, but that made no sense at all based on the conversation he'd heard. They had definitely been thinking of the task of corpse and evidence disposal as more than a one-person job. Also, both had been so wired and on-edge it was impossible to believe either could have lapsed into sleep just a few minutes later.

So who the hell was this mystery sleeper?

He guessed it was someone who'd entered the house with Bree and Slick just a little while ago, but for whatever reason whoever it was had not been expected to participate in the bloody cleanup work. There could be many reasons for that and he could speculate about them endlessly without ever pinpointing the right one. It didn't matter. The bottom line was this—could he slip past this person and exit the house without waking him or her up?

From his vantage point, he could see most of the living room. He saw the coffee table, the debris-strewn floor, the television, and the stereo system. The only thing he couldn't fully glimpse was the sofa. By leaning forward, he was able to see a foot in a pink ankle sock hanging over the edge of the sofa. The sock told him there was a high likelihood the sleeper was a woman. That sexist part of him he usually worked so hard to suppress also helpfully suggested he could probably take a woman in a confrontation, if it came down to that.

Johnny nonetheless had quite a quandary on his hands. The way he saw it he had two options. He could continue down the stairs as quietly as he could manage and then hope to slip out of the house without the woman waking up and spotting him. Or he could retreat again to the bedroom and open the window in there. The prospect of climbing out the window and dropping to the ground below wasn't one he relished. A neighbor might spot him and figure him for a burglar making a getaway, for one thing. But the thing that really worried him about that option was the possibility of breaking something when he hit the ground. It wouldn't be a huge drop from the second-floor window, but it would be so easy to land wrong and twist or break something—and that would be fucking disastrous.

Johnny hesitated on the verge of decision several more moments, all the while aware of an invisible clock ticking. The longer he fidgeted and did nothing, the stronger the likelihood of disaster regardless of which option he chose.

Fuck it.

He let out a breath and started down the stairs again, keeping a hand solidly on the banister to reduce the odds of an inadvertent tumble. This proved a brilliant move seconds later as the sleeping woman came into view. She was lying on her side facing the back of the sofa, but the shape of the woman's body told him everything.

Lily!

"Holy fucking Jesus…"

He immediately regretted verbalizing his shock, because even in the midst of shock he recognized it as a potentially fatal mistake, but he was simply unable to help himself. It didn't matter that he couldn't see her face. Every instinct he had—and all of his senses—told him the irrefutable truth of it. And now that he was seeing her again, he was stunned to think he'd ever mistaken that other woman—*that poor dead woman*, he reminded himself—for his ex-wife. The memory of how her body felt snuggled against his came back to him with shocking force, momentarily robbing him of his breath. He remembered the supple smoothness of her flawless skin, the soft texture of her hair when he ran his fingers through it, and he remembered all the lines and little contours of every part of her body with painful clarity.

He wiped moisture from his eyes.

God, he was so fucking glad she was alive.

But once the initial shock of the moment passed, he was left with a boatload of deeply troubling questions. The big one, of course, was how much Lily knew about what had happened to the woman who'd gotten her face erased with a hammer. And right after that—what role, if any, had she played in the murder?

Lily had changed a lot and had behaved in ways he didn't understand since the dissolution of their marriage, but not for one second did he believe she was capable of something so heinous. He guessed maybe she'd known about it after-the-fact, which possibly explained the condition Nora had seen her in at the grocery store. The murder perpetrated by her friends had so upset her that she'd opted to drink herself into a falling-down stupor rather than deal with it. As far as coping mechanisms went, it was one Johnny understood all too well.

He descended the remaining stairs and crossed the living room to the sofa, treading lightly and taking care to avoid stepping on any of the party detritus. When he reached the sofa, Lily stirred and shifted position slightly, groaning and stretching her legs out a little. But then she sucked in another big breath and kept right on sleeping. The reek of booze rolled off her in waves pungent enough to have gagged a skid row bum.

Again, he stood on the point of indecision longer than prudent. Whatever Lily's actual role in things had been, she was wrapped up in it all somehow. Yes, she was drunk as hell, but she had been left unattended. She wasn't being held prisoner. Obviously Bree and Slick trusted her not to go blabbing about the murder to the police. Johnny struggled with an urge to rouse her and drag her out of this place. He could go to Joe Voss and maybe some strings could be pulled, some kind of deal arranged that would keep her out of jail in exchange for ratting out her friends. That kind of shit happened all the time on cop shows. But this wasn't the pretend world of television. Who knew how that kind of shit would actually work in reality, or if it was even possible? And that wasn't even factoring in the very real chance that she would react negatively—possibly even violently—to his presence here.

While Johnny thought it over, he noted Lily *had* gotten some tattoos since he'd seen her last, including one of a thorny vine that traversed the length of one hip and disappeared under her cotton shorts, presumably continuing up the side of her body.

He wished he could see the rest of it. It was a bittersweet desire, because he knew it was a wish she would never grant him.

He bent toward her, extending a hand toward her shoulder.

This was an unconscious act, one he instantly knew he should abort. He shouldn't wake her. She didn't want his help. His mind screamed reminders of these probable facts at him even as his hand touched her shoulder. She stirred at his touch, groaning again in her sleep. His eyes watered again. God, how he'd longed for physical contact with her over the many long months since she'd walked out of his life.

When he looked back on it later, he knew he would have gone through with the questionable and impulsive decision to wake her given the chance. But he heard a car pull up outside in the very next moment and the sound of it sent him running to the back of the house. This was another thing that happened on pure instinct. The car might well have belonged to a resident from the other side of the duplex. It was a more likely explanation than a premature return of Bree and Slick.

One second he had his hand on her shoulder and the next he was running, simple as that. In his haste he banged a hip against the edge of the cluttered kitchen table and sent some empty beer bottles tumbling to the floor, where they shattered on the linoleum. Johnny never slowed down. He hauled the back door open and ran as fast as his feet would take him across the back yard to the thin line of trees beyond.

9

The cab dropped Johnny off at the curb outside the Delirium Lounge. As always, he over-tipped the driver. The driver thanked him and sped away. Johnny spotted a folded sheet of paper clipped to the Austin-Healey's windshield beneath a wiper blade. He grabbed it on the way in and shoved it into a pocket.

The Delirium Lounge was more crowded than when he'd left it, which was typical for the hour. The after-work crowd was here and there was a louder buzz of conversation and laughter. He was lucky to find an open stool at the bar.

The bartender set a Maker's Mark double in front of him before he'd fully settled himself on the stool. Johnny gulped it down fast and threw a twenty dollar bill on the bar, which was not-so-secret code for "keep 'em coming."

After fleeing the duplex, he'd emerged through the line of trees into someone else's back yard, where a snarling pit bull chained to a stake had leapt at him and nearly sent him scurrying back the way he'd come. But the animal reached the fullest extension of the chain a yard or so shy of Johnny's vulnerable crotch. He was able to avoid death-by-fangs by moving away from the pit bull in a careful arc until he reached the side of the house, where he took off running. When he reached the next street over, he used his cell phone to summon a cab and now here he was. Not even a full half hour had passed since his escape from the scene of the crime. He checked his watch. Hell, it was barely more than twenty minutes ago. And his heart was still beating way too fast.

Johnny knocked back his second double whiskey in one go. He'd come into the bar stone sober, the afternoon's largish influx of booze burned away by all the terror and excitement. Staying sober was not an option after all that had gone down. Lily being alive complicated everything. When he'd believed she was dead, his course had been more or less clear—get the cops involved as soon as possible and send the bad guys to the slammer. But now that option was off the table, at least for the time being.

His ex-wife was in this mess up to her eyeballs. He didn't like the idea of Bree and Slick avoiding justice, but he also didn't care for the idea of Lily going to jail. Nor could he stomach the notion of being the one to send her there. So that left, what, keeping quiet about what he'd seen?

He grimaced and signaled for another drink..

Jesus, am I seriously thinking of letting these people get away with murder?

Apparently a big part of him was considering that very thing, even though the idea of it was twisting his stomach up in knots and making him feel nauseated.

The bartender—a young guy named Mick with a mop of wavy brown hair—set a third Maker's Mark double on the bar. He then leaned across the bar to make his voice audible above the din of conversation. "Did you get the note from Nora?"

Johnny frowned. "Note?"

Mick nodded. "Yeah, man. She said she was leaving it on your car. Said you should be sure to call her as soon as you got back. She was real adamant about that."

Johnny's frown deepened. "I don't remember any...oh, wait."

He'd assumed the folded sheet of paper clipped to his windshield was a flyer for some lame local band, this being a college town with far more than its fair quota of lame-ass bands who liked to paper the square with their fucking flyers, but obviously it was Nora's note.

He dug the sheet of paper out of his pocket and unfolded it. It had a few choice words for him regarding his abrupt departure, including some that were underlined multiple times, which struck Johnny as excessive. The gist of it was twofold—he hadn't shown her proper consideration by bolting without explanation, and he was a fool for not letting go of his feelings for Lily. The way Johnny saw it, the latter was an unnecessary reiteration of what she'd told him earlier. As for the other part of it, why did he owe her an explanation for anything? It wasn't as if they'd been on a date.

The note closed with an all-caps *demand* that he call her just as soon as he was able.

Well…fuck that.

He liked Nora, but the last thing he needed was another headache. He couldn't stomach the idea of being yelled at by a pissed-off woman while his head was roiling with so many conflicting thoughts about what he'd seen and endured. Johnny belatedly realized a third double whiskey was already in front of him. He made it go away and signaled for yet another.

Mick poured it for him, but this time he had a mildly troubled look on his face. "Drowning your sorrows, Johnny?"

"Don't go getting all judgmental on me. Helping people drown their sorrows is your goddamn job."

Mick shrugged. "No judgment here, Johnny. You can drink yourself blind for all I care, but that Austin-Healey stays here tonight. You get me?"

"I get you." Johnny sipped from his latest Maker's Mark. "I'll call a cab. You know, like I do half the time anyway?"

Mick's expression turned thoughtful. "I really think you should call Nora."

"She pay you to say that?"

"I just know how hard it can be to let go of something before you're ready." Mick's usual air of aloof amusement had vanished and in its place was a plain sincerity that made Johnny wary. "I got dumped by a girl I fucking worshipped and I spent

months moping around like a pitiful lost soul. Then one day I
met this other girl--"

"And like *that!*" Johnny snapped his fingers, making
Mick flinch. "You were magically all better. Right?"

Mick gave his head a weary shake. "Go ahead, be a dick
if you want, I don't care. No, I didn't magically get better, but
you knew that already. I'll tell you what, though. It was the
start of something. I never had sex with that girl again, but there
were some more one night stands after that. And then a little
later on I started seeing another girl regularly. That's how it is,
man. You just gotta get back in the saddle. Life's short. It
keeps moving ahead even when you're standing still. If you're
not careful, it'll all be over and you'll wind up wondering what
the fuck happened."

"That's some profound shit."

Mick grabbed a couple bottles from the shelves behind
him and began mixing up another customer's drink order. "Profound is my middle name, buddy."

"Huh. I thought your middle name was Ass-face."

Mick chuckled. "That's what I love about booze. Get
enough drinks in any man and he reverts back to an eighth grade
sense of humor."

"Whatever, Ass-face."

Mick chuckled again and moved off to take another drink
order.

After polishing off his fourth double whiskey, Johnny
tossed another twenty on the bar. He walked out of the Delirium
Lounge and paused on the sidewalk outside to light up a cigarillo. The sun was beginning its slow slide toward the horizon.
The accompanying slight drop in temperature made him feel a
little better. Cloying heat made it harder to get his thoughts in
order. Of course, an impartial observer might suggest the booze
was really to blame, but it was Johnny's considered opinion that
this theoretical observer could fuck off.

Johnny moved down the block a little until he came to a
sidewalk bench. He sat and smoked his cigarillo, watching the

human and vehicular traffic stream by as he tried to figure out what to do next. He knew what he wanted to do. He wanted to get blotto. That had been his original intention upon entering the Delirium Lounge, but Mick and his irritatingly sensible words had derailed the impulse.

This was a serious situation he was in, to understate.

If he didn't take some kind of action today, he might wind up keeping quiet about it forever. Oh, he wouldn't want to do that and his conscience would continue to eat at him, but the urgency would fade and ultimately disappear if he allowed days to slip away while he remained mired in indecision. His fierce reluctance to do anything that would get Lily in serious trouble would make that even more likely to happen.

Johnny smoked the cigarillo down to a stub and flicked it into the storm drain at the curb. He lit up another one and smoked it all the way down, too. Thoughts on the dilemma facing him kept circling around in his head without making any positive progress in any direction, even after the effects of the whiskeys began to lift some. It was frustrating enough that he found himself on the verge of heading across the street to 3 Brothers Craft Brewhouse, where he could resume getting hammered without a friend's good intentions to sour things.

Instead he pulled out his phone and made a call.

Nora answered on the first ring. "You better be calling to apologize."

"That's part of it." Johnny sighed wearily. "I'd like to see you."

"So come see me."

Johnny cast a longing gaze in the direction of the Austin-Healey. "The thing is, I'm not quite fit to drive. Could you come pick me up?"

"You're drunk."

Her tone wasn't one of accusation. Not quite. It wasn't the shrewish voice of a nag. She was just stating a fact, the same way she would say, *The sky is blue.* You couldn't take offense at it, not really, but something in Johnny rankled at it anyway.

For a moment he considered ending the call, but he recognized the impulse as the usual self-destructive crap and shut it down.

"Not quite, but I'm not exactly fit to drive, either."

"You can come see me, Johnny, but I'm not your personal chauffeur. Call a cab."

She gave him an address and hung up.

Johnny stared blankly at the phone a moment before putting it away. He then looked across the street at 3 Brothers. Live music emanated from that direction, some local band playing. The music was bluesy and the singer had a soulful voice that could rise to the thrilling kind of eardrum-rattling but perfectly tuneful scream Janis Joplin had done so well. They didn't sound half-bad. There were young people hanging out and smoking cigarettes on the sidewalk outside the bar.

He could still go over there. It would be a good time.

And he could forget about everything for a while, just drink and drink until it all went away, at least until he came to in the morning at some as-yet-undetermined location with an epic hangover and an even bigger sense of regret.

Johnny got up and hailed a cab.

10

Johnny experienced a jolt of disorientation when his eyes fluttered open at two in the morning. He had been dreaming about the nameless girl with the bashed-in face. The dream faded to fragmented fuzziness as soon as his eyes were open, but a few troubling images lingered, as did a vague sense of guilt. In the dream the dead girl became a walking corpse. She slithered off the bed and staggered over to the closet, seeming somehow to know Johnny was hiding inside it. She clawed at the door and made a series of horrible, moist sounds, noises that were almost words. The hammer that had killed her was clutched in Johnny's trembling right hand.

When he woke up, he had a faint sense that he was not where he belonged. Though it was dark, he could discern outlines of unfamiliar objects, including things that might have been bookshelves where he was not accustomed to seeing bookshelves. The bookshelves in his home were in his office rather than in the bedroom. Also, the texture of the sheets beneath his naked body felt far softer than his own sheets. When he realized there was another human being curled up asleep next to him, it came back to him that he was in bed with Nora Lewis in her home. The glowing digital clock on the nightstand to his left told him more than an hour had passed since they'd drifted off to sleep together after making love.

So he'd gotten laid.

He smiled in the dark, thinking about how Mick would be proud of him.

That strange sense of guilt lingered a few more minutes. He knew it was just his subconscious mixing up a lot of stray thoughts regarding the previous day's troubling events and rearranging them in a nonsensical new pattern while adding in a big extra dose of the horrific and surreal. Having bad dreams during times of stress was a perfectly ordinary phenomenon. In Johnny's experience, however, a large influx of alcohol prior to sleep had a way of cranking up the weird and disturbing aspects of nightmares, often rendering them so vivid they felt real for a short while after consciousness returned.

I'm not the one who bashed in that girl's face, he reminded himself. *I'm not a bad guy at all. I'm just—*

Johnny frowned.

He was just a guy who had witnessed a violent crime—its aftermath, anyway—and had done nothing about it. The girl with the ruined face must have died in agony. He hadn't known her, but he couldn't pretend she wasn't real. She was more than just the unpleasant centerpiece in a clusterfuck of a situation that threatened to ruin his ex-wife's life. Somewhere out there were people who had loved her and would soon be missing her. He imagined a mother marking a passage of years, never giving up hope her daughter would one day call or come home. It was the kind of story you saw on the news all the time. Most of those missing kids never came home and faceless girl wouldn't be any different.

But if Johnny could just find it within himself to do the right thing…

He sat up and swung his legs over the side of the bed. His mind was racing in a way that would make falling asleep again nigh impossible, at least for a while. A deeper sleep would come easier in his own bed, especially if he allowed himself a few medicinal shots of whiskey first. He could leave Nora a note thanking her for a wonderful night and promising to call her later in the day. Given his state of mind, it felt like his best option. He might even have acted on the idea, except he remembered his Austin-Healey was elsewhere. Yeah, he could call yet another cab, but suddenly it seemed like too much trouble. And the longer he sat there without acting, the harder it was to get away from another unpleasant fact—if Nora woke up later this morning and he wasn't here, she would be furious.

There was no commitment between them. He didn't owe her anything beyond what had happened tonight, but Nora had been kind to him despite his rudeness earlier. She deserved better than to be treated like just another one night stand. So in the end he abandoned the notion of slipping away. However, that still left him with the problem of what to do about his racing, troubled mind.

A drink would help.

Johnny grunted.

A drink *always* helped.

Pulling on boxer shorts, he stumbled out of the bedroom to the hallway beyond, where he made a side trip to the bathroom to relieve an overburdened bladder. After flushing, he searched the medicine cabinet and found a little bottle of generic acetaminophen. He popped a handful into his mouth and washed them down with cold water from the tap. When he closed the medicine cabinet's door, he was unable to look his reflection in the eye. This made him feel cowardly and small and reinforced the notion that a few wee hours drinks were absolutely vital.

After making his way out to the kitchen in the dark, he turned on the light above the stove so he could see better and opened Nora's refrigerator. He saw a few bottles of blueberry wheat beer and a lone bottle of Budweiser. There was also a bottle of wine in one of the door racks. Johnny liked beer. He was a guy. Liking beer was sort of required if you didn't want your Man Card torn up. But his preferences when it came to suds were not reflected in the available selection. What he really wanted was that bottle of wine, but he had a strong hunch finding that gone was another thing that wouldn't make Nora the least bit happy. So he opted for the Budweiser as a temporary solution and decided he'd search the cupboards for liquor.

He had downed most of the bottle of Bud and had searched nearly all the cupboards when the overhead florescent light popped on, making him jump. He shut the door on a cupboard crammed with canned goods and turned around to see Nora entering the kitchen.

"Oh. Hey."

Nora was starkers, as the Brits used to say. The sight of her nude body momentarily befuddled him, but then it came back to him that he'd very recently spent some quality time engaged in sexual congress with that body and his brain resumed something resembling normal functionality. The downside of this was that now he could see how annoyed she looked.

"What are you looking for, Johnny?"

"Um, well…" *Might as well spit it out.* "Booze, frankly."

Nora gave him a blank look for a moment. Then she rolled her eyes and approached a door in a corner of the kitchen. A pantry was behind the door. Johnny felt some relief as he watched her poke around inside it. He'd glimpsed the faintest hint of a smile before she'd turned away from him. Maybe he wasn't about to get a rasher of shit from her, after all.

She shut the door and showed him bottles of Knob Creek whiskey and Absolut vodka.

Johnny smiled. "I think I'm in love."

Nora gave him a sour look. "Grab us some glasses, you fucking lush. Make mine a martini glass."

While he did as instructed, Nora set the bottles on the counter and opened the refrigerator. She reached inside it and took out a lemon and a bottle of vermouth. Next she opened a drawer and Johnny heard a rattling of cutlery as she searched for a paring knife. She found one and began to peel the lemon on a cutting board.

Johnny opened the freezer and added some ice cubes to the whiskey glass. He filled it with three fingers of Knob Creek and took a sip. The sweet burn of quality whiskey lit up his taste buds and filled him with the usual warm glow. He sighed in gratitude. "I'm sorry if I woke you up."

Nora shrugged as she finished preparing her vodka martini. "I'm surprised you're still here. I was sure you'd slipped away while I was asleep."

Johnny grimaced. "I have to admit the idea occurred to me, but…"

She glanced at him. "But you decided not to be an asshole?"

He shrugged and had another sip of whiskey. "Something like that."

"Well, good for you. Come on, we'll drink out on the deck."

Johnny grabbed the bottle of Knob Creek and followed her to the French doors at the other end of the kitchen. When they were outside, they sat in wrought-iron chairs at a wrought-iron table. A tall wooden umbrella stand protruded from a hole in the center of the table, but the umbrella was closed. The cool air made for a refreshing change from the cloying heat of the previous day.

Nora took a contemplative sip of her martini and leaned back in her chair. "Cards on the table time, Johnny."

Johnny reflexively tensed. He didn't like the sound of that.

Nora smiled. "I'm sure you don't like the sound of that."

Johnny kept his face carefully blank.

Oh my God, she can read my mind. I have to get out of here.

Nora laughed. "You look like the proverbial kid caught with his hand in the cookie jar."

Johnny's laugh felt forced. "Um…"

"I'm just gonna lay this on you, Johnny. Life's short and I don't feel like fucking around." She fixed him with the deadly serious gaze of a doctor about to deliver life-changing news. "I like you, Johnny, and more than just a little. I have for a long time. I couldn't do anything about it while you were with Lily and after you two split I knew you needed space and time. But it's been over a year and it's time you started really living your life again."

Johnny sighed. "People keep telling me that."

"Well, you should listen to them. And you should listen to me now, because I'm going to be blunt. Lily never really appreciated you. She took advantage of you and when she was done having her fun with you, she dumped you like yesterday's garbage."

Johnny winced. "Harsh."

"It's the truth."

Johnny didn't say anything. It *was* the truth. At least it was part of the truth. It reflected how things had been in the last couple years of the relationship. Those first several years were another story. She had really loved him then. He *knew* she had.

Nora smiled sadly. "You need to quit trying to figure it out. It's done. Figuring out the rest of your life is what you should be focused on now."

Johnny took a big sip of whiskey. "Look…I like you, too, Nora. You're a cool chick. Beautiful, smart, the whole package. And I get everything you're saying. I just think I'm still not ready for anything serious."

"Relax, Johnny. This isn't an ultimatum. I'm not expecting you to propose marriage after one night of incredible sex." Nora laughed and grinned at him over the rim of her glass. "Let's change gears. Something's been bugging you all night. You want to talk about it?"

Johnny tilted his head back and peered up at the dark sky above for a long moment. The moon was luminous and lovely, there was a low buzz of insects mating in the tall trees at the back of the yard, and somewhere a dog was barking intermittently. The peacefulness of the setting felt at odds with the dark cloud hanging over him.

He gave Nora a grim look and said, "I saw something today. Something terrible. I'll tell you about it, but before I do, I need you to promise you won't breathe a word of it to anybody. I mean it, Nora. I need your solemn fucking vow."

She gave him a long, searching look before responding. "Okay, Johnny. I promise. Unless you say otherwise, I'll take whatever it is to my grave. I solemnly fucking swear."

Johnny knocked back the rest of the whiskey in his glass and filled it again from the bottle.

And then he told her everything.

11

Several hours later Nora dropped Johnny off outside the Delirium Lounge so he could pick up the Austin-Healey. His plan was to head straight home and stay in until Nora got off work later in the day. She was only doing a half day thanks to their long, occasionally contentious early morning conversation. The only reason she'd gone in at all was because there were some things requiring her attention that simply couldn't be postponed. But she had made it clear she wanted him to stay sober until they could resume discussion of The Lily Situation. That was how he thought of it now, in capital letters, to denote its suddenly massive significance in his life. So he had promised her he wouldn't drink until she was able to swing by his house after work.

But the call of the Delirium Lounge was strong. It was a few minutes after noon, which meant the bar had just opened. He could have the place almost to himself for a while. Maybe it would be okay if he just went in and nursed a beer or two. Staying off the hard stuff ought to keep him out of trouble.

Johnny jingled his keys in nervous anticipation. He closed his eyes, took a deep breath, and counted slowly to ten. When he opened them again, the intensity of the urge had diminished, though it hadn't entirely gone away, which he doubted anything short of death could accomplish. So he got in the Austin-Healey, fired up the engine, and backed out of the parking space before it could become overpowering.

On the drive home, he reflected on his frank talk with Nora and her reaction to his "confession". She had tried hard to refrain from being judgmental, which he appreciated, but it was clear she was less than happy with him. She agreed he was in a difficult situation, but it was largely the fault of his inability to recognize that Lily's life was her own now and that he had no business sticking his nose in her affairs.

He didn't want to further damage her impression of him by failing to honor a simple promise. Besides, how hard could staying sober a measly few hours be? He just had to refrain from boozing it up until they could have a relatively clear-headed conversation about the situation, which Johnny figured was fair enough. All he had to do was make it through the next few hours. Surely he couldn't manage that.

On the whole, he guessed he had to be grateful she hadn't completely lost her shit when he got into some of the more gruesome details of The Lily Situation. A part of him had been sure she would do just that. This was definitely a losing-your-shit kind of situation no matter how you looked at it. Many of his closest associates and friends who wouldn't have handled the news anywhere near as calmly, regardless of any promises to the contrary they might have made beforehand. It spoke to an overall levelheadedness on her part. Having an influence like that in his life on an ongoing basis might not be such a bad thing.

Whoa. Hold on.

What was he thinking here? That pursuing a relationship with Nora might actually be a good idea? Getting into anything serious with another woman was something he'd sworn to himself he would avoid at all costs for the foreseeable future. Not just because he wasn't over Lily, but because falling in love was dangerous. It would mean making himself emotionally vulnerable again and that was the last thing he wanted.

Johnny frowned as he turned down the street leading to his house.

But he liked her.

Dammit.

He *really* liked her.

He was suddenly unable to hide from a simple truth. At some point over the course of their long night together, she had begun to get under his skin. Something clicked. It was on a level so subtle he hadn't been aware it was happening at first. And by the time he *did* realize it was happening, it was too late to follow his usual impulse to run and hide.

Thoughts of Nora and what the future might hold slid away as Johnny neared his Victorian-style house in Murfreesboro's historic district. The house was old but had been renovated in the 1980's. It was a nice home with a lot of character that had cost him a pretty penny during more prosperous days, and he hoped to be able to hang on to it.

But right now he was more interested in what was in the driveway.

An old Honda Civic.

Lily's car.

12

The shock of seeing Lily's car in his driveway more than a year after she'd last set foot in his house temporarily paralyzed Johnny. He sat in his car with his foot on the brake for a long moment. During that moment, he was in a kind of fog. But then the world snapped back into focus and he was briefly possessed by a powerful urge to step on the gas and keep on driving. He hadn't yet turned into the driveway. It would be easy enough to zip on by without being noticed. But that wouldn't remain the case if he lingered here much longer.

Lily being back at his house after so long away—and just a day after he'd let himself into her place and seen what he'd seen—couldn't be a coincidence. There was no such thing as coincidence that big, at least not in Johnny's experience. Somehow yesterday's events and Lily's presence here today were connected.

But no one had been aware of his presence while he was in the duplex. There were a lot of things he wasn't sure of lately, but that wasn't one of them. He'd eluded detection thanks to Lily's drunken stupor and the obliviousness of Bree and Slick.

He was sure of it.

So...what the hell?

There was no one in the Civic so far as Johnny could tell. He frowned as he recalled something potentially significant. In the early stages of their breakup, he'd told Lily she was welcome to come home whenever she was ready. He had refused to take her key when she offered it to him and had never changed the locks. Doing that would have been one of those final cutting of the ties things that are so hard to do when you've had your heart broken.

But now he was regretting it because there was a good chance Lily was in his house right now. What would have been welcome news not so long ago was now something that caused him great anxiety. The impulse to drive away lessened as he thought about what she might be doing in there. He had seen firsthand the squalor she lived in. She might be desperate and looking for something to steal. He owned a lot of valuable things, so it was plausible.

The smart thing would be to drive away and come back after she was done looting the place. Material items could be replaced. He didn't care too much if she took them. Feeling briefly decisive, he took his foot off the brake and the Austin-Healey rolled forward a few feet. But he stepped on the brake again when he thought of the potentially sensitive stuff on his laptop, not the least of which was the key to his Facebook identity as Joanna Walker. His gut clenched at the thought.

Johnny turned into the driveway and parked the Austin-Healey next to Lily's car. He got out and peeked inside the Civic. As he'd suspected, there was no one in it. The car's interior was littered with junk. Much of it was concentrated in the back, where Lily had tossed innumerable crumpled fast food bags and empty soda bottles. There were more than a few empty beer bottles, as well. The mess puzzled Johnny. She had always kept her Lexus spotless, had almost been anal about it. It was difficult not to see the mess as indicative of an overall state of chaos in her life. Seeing it stirred anew that instinctive protectiveness that had sent him running to her place yesterday. She was in a bad situation and he should do whatever he could to help her get out of it. This thought was followed almost immediately by a keen awareness of what Nora would have to say about that.

Johnny went into his house and found Lily waiting for him in the spacious living room. Classical music was playing softly on the stereo system. Hearing it triggered a wave of goose bump-raising nostalgia, bringing to mind countless times when he'd come home from some errand to find Lily relaxing in the living room while enjoying a glass of wine and listening to her favorite composers. Johnny didn't much care for classical. He was your stereotypical classic rock kind of guy who would sometimes also listen to a bit of modern Americana. This was the first time Beethoven had been heard within the walls of his home in—wait for it—over a year.

The remains of a six-pack of Miller High Life sat atop the cherrywood coffee table. Two full cans were still attached to the plastic binder. There were some crumpled empties beside them. Lily was dressed in tight denim cutoffs and a sleeveless blue halter top. She was barefoot, her brown pumps tossed aside on the floor. Aside from the tattoos and the somewhat sluttier attire, she looked much as he remembered.

She sat cross-legged on the long sectional, his laptop open in her lap. Johnny couldn't help cringing at this realization of his worst fears.

Shit.

She glanced up at him as he came into the room, her expression conveying no sense of a person who wasn't where she belonged. "Who the fuck is Joanna Walker?"

Ah, fuck.

Johnny hesitated only for a moment, during which he was certain he would go on gaping at her like an idiot until the truth behind his Facebook ruse became painfully clear. But then a potentially convincing lie—one almost beautifully pure in its simplicity—came to him. By the time the words were out of his mouth, he was surprised he hadn't had this exact cover story cooked up in advance of this inevitability.

"Just this girl I was seeing for a while." He shrugged. "What are you doing, looking at her Facebook page?"

Lily's eyes slitted in a vaguely distrustful way as she appeared to gauge both his demeanor and the veracity of what he'd told her. Then a sneer tugged at a side of her mouth as she shook her head. "Let me guess. You had her friend me and

Bree so you could keep tabs on us. That's some sneaky fucking bullshit."

Johnny sighed. "I know. I'm sorry."

"I guess the bitch never changes her password." She grunted as her forefinger moved over the laptop's touchpad. "How convenient for you. I checked your browsing history. You look at our pages a lot. But whatever. I've unfriended her and I'll get Bree to do the same."

She closed the laptop and set it on the coffee table.

Johnny frowned. "What are you doing here?"

"I decided it was time to come home. You said I could come back whenever I was ready, right?" Lily shrugged. "Well, here I am. Aren't you happy?"

Johnny was at a total loss as to what to say. If Lily had shown up here asking the same question just twenty-four hours ago, his answer would have been an unhesitating yes. But things had changed and he was no longer sure what he wanted. Some of his long-held perceptions of his ex-wife had changed in what felt like fundamentally irreversible ways.

And yet…

God, she's still so damn beautiful.

It was true.

And despite everything—all he'd seen yesterday and all the ways she'd changed—his intense desire for her was still there. His eyes drank in all the familiar sweet curves of her body and he was almost overcome by an aching need to touch and caress her.

Lily patted the cushion next to her. "Sit down, Johnny. Let's have a drink and talk things out."

Johnny took a half-step toward the sofa and hesitated. He couldn't allow Lily to exert her old power over him, regardless of how tempting it was to just surrender. He had a hunch she meant to fuck him, knowing full well being intimate with her again after so long would make him vulnerable and suggestible.

"Lily…you need to leave."

She laughed. "What? Are you serious?"

He sighed. "Yeah. I guess I am."

Lily got up from the sofa and approached him. She walked in a hip-swaying, exaggeratedly sexy way. Watching her move like that inflamed the desire he was trying to fight back. She was slightly wobbly, though, thanks to the beers she'd consumed, which somewhat diminished the effect she was trying to achieve. Johnny nonetheless tensed and held his breath as she put her arms around his neck and pressed herself against him.

She fluttered her eyelids and sighed. "You can have me right here if you want. Tear my clothes off and throw me down on the floor. Come on, Johnny. I know you want it."

Johnny closed his eyes and groaned.

Want it? Baby, that's the understatement of the goddamn century.

He opened his eyes, reached behind his neck, and peeled her hands away from him. He took a few deliberate steps back and put some steel in his voice when he spoke again. "I want you to leave. The offer I made after you left has expired. This isn't your home anymore. Please go."

The seductive playfulness leeched out of Lily's expression, exposing an open hostility Johnny understood had been right under the surface the whole time. "I'm here because I need help and I thought you of all people would be willing to give it to me. You told me you'd love me forever and do anything for me. I guess that was a lie, huh, Johnny?"

Johnny grunted. "I did say those things. But that was a while ago and things have changed."

"Is it that Joanna bitch? Are you hung up on her?"

Johnny almost laughed at that but managed to restrain the urge. "She's...out of the picture now."

Lily studied his face for a moment before scowling and nodding. "But someone else is *in* the picture, right? Don't lie to me, asshole. Admit it. You're banging some other whore now."

Johnny's first impulse was to deny it. He didn't want to get into this with her. All he wanted was Lily gone from his life for good, a development shocking in its suddenness but also galvanizing in how right it felt. It was liberating. A psychic weight had lifted from him and until this moment he hadn't fully appreciated how heavy a burden it had been.

"You're right. I am seeing someone else. And you know what? She treats me decently and doesn't take me for granted. And there ain't any way I'd ditch her to take up with the likes of you again."

"What's this perfect little angel's fucking name?"

"None of your business."

Lily glared at him, the hate and contempt rolling off her in palpable waves. It was disturbing how nakedly she was displaying her true feelings now. Johnny had a memory flash of the nameless girl's brutalized body and felt a stab of genuine fear. It was important to remember that this was a woman who willingly associated with lowlifes. The part of him that still had feelings for her wanted to believe she couldn't possibly be a genuine threat to his personal safety. However, his inner pragmatist knew that was far from a safe assumption.

She shook her head. "Whatever. It's not like I really care who you're fucking now. I just feel sorry for her, whoever she is, for having to put up with your boring ass. You need to give me some money, Johnny."

"What?"

"You heard me."

Johnny laughed. "Why would I give you money?"

"If you don't, I'll call the cops and tell them you lured me here and tried to rape me."

Johnny gaped at her in disbelief. "You're shitting me."

Lily's smile had a mean edge to it. "I'm not shitting you. And we both know how convincing an actress I can be."

Johnny didn't need this kind of drama. Not now or ever. Sure, he could maybe stick it to her by telling the responding officers about what he'd seen at Lily's duplex, but that would amount to inviting a thousand times more drama and strife into his life. There would be repercussions small and large, all of them adding up to a titanic pain in the ass. In truth, the possibility of telling the cops about what he'd seen was a ship that had already sailed, a fact he was only now fully accepting.

So he would give her the money. It was now painfully obvious money was what she'd been after all along, which explained her coincidental presence here in a way that made sense. She was broke and probably unemployed. Hitting up the relatively moneyed ex had been inevitable. Well, she could have what she was after this time, but after this they were done for good as far as he was concerned. He would do whatever was necessary to make that happen. One of his first orders of business would be to call a damn locksmith.

"Wait here. I'll be right back."

Lily smirked. "I'm not going anywhere."

Johnny left the living room and navigated the maze of hallways in his big house until he arrived at his office. There was a heavy combination safe on one of the bookshelves. The safe was new, which was a good thing. Lily likely would have helped herself to its contents already otherwise. He spun the dial and opened the safe. Inside were stacks of emergency cash, his passport, and a loaded 9mm handgun. He picked up one of the banded cash stacks and peeled off ten one-hundred dollar bills.

He returned to the living room and handed over the cash.

Lily counted the bills and glared at him. "A lousy grand? Really? That's not enough, Johnny."

Johnny shrugged. "That's all you're getting. You can either take it and be happy you got something or you can make good on your threat to call the police, in which case you get nothing. It's up to you."

She was still angry, but he saw the defeat in her face. "I fucking hate you. You know that?"

Johnny nodded. "I guess I do. I don't get it, but I don't care anymore either. It's time for you to go."

Still seething, Lily stomped across the living room to retrieve her shoes and leftover beers. Once she had accomplished these things, Johnny followed her out of the house, stopping in his tracks when she abruptly spun about on the porch and faced him again. For a moment, her face remained a mask of rage.

But then a strange thing happened.

She removed the big movie-star sunglasses hooked over the top of her halter and slid them on. Her face transformed, a stunning smile curving the corners of her pouty lips.

"I know you were there yesterday, Johnny."

Johnny's heart almost stopped at these words.

Lily laughed and turned away from him to descend the steps to the sidewalk. She ran to her car and waved to him when she reached the door. "Bye, Johnny! See you soon!"

Johnny at last managed to speak. "Wait--"

But Lily was already in her car. She backed out of the driveway and sped away.

Johnny stood there gaping out at the empty street for many long minutes, feeling dazed and extremely confused.

His head was spinning and he again couldn't make any sense out of anything.

So he went inside and had a drink.

13

The drink flew out of Johnny's hand when Nora's hand cracked across his face. This was no half-hearted blow. There was serious force behind it. The glass shattered on the hard-wood floor as Johnny staggered back a step. He felt a twinge of regret when he glimpsed the little puddle on the floor. It looked sort of inconsequential, but that was a good two ounces of pre-mium whiskey gone to waste. A shame, but he had bigger things to worry about at the moment.

Nora's face had turned a shade of furious scarlet. "You promised, Johnny!"

Johnny's face still stung from the ringing slap. He gently touched his inflamed cheek and winced. "I know, okay? And no one's sorrier than I am. I had every intention of staying true to my word, but something happened and the stress of it got to me."

Nora's furious expression turned appraising, which Johnny took as a hopeful sign. All women had an inner ability to sniff out deceit to some degree, but a few were almost super-naturally talented in that area. Nora likely fell into that category. He could only hope she would see he was telling her nothing but the plain truth.

She sighed. "You better tell me all about it."

"Sure. But let's sit down first."

Nora nodded and they sat next to each other on the sofa.

He had disposed of Lily's empty Miller High Life cans, but now he was thinking he should have left them out as visual evidence to back up his story. But this was a fleeting thought that went away the moment he started telling Nora about his encounter with Lily. Visual evidence wasn't necessary when you had a story as compellingly sordid as this one.

He related the tale as methodically as possible, describing nearly everything that had happened in detail and occasionally quoting Lily word-for-word. The only thing he left out was her discovery of the fake Joanna Walker Facebook page. Johnny wanted to be honest, but that didn't mean he shouldn't judiciously edit out things that might not reflect well on him. And he had a feeling Nora would see through the cover story he'd fooled Lily with in about two seconds flat.

Nora looked pale when the story was concluded. "My God, Johnny."

"I know. It's fucked up."

She shook her head. "Jesus. I think I need a drink now."

"What would you like?"

She had been staring off into a middle distance, but now she cut her eyes at him. "Vodka martini. But you should refrain a while. We've got some serious things to discuss and I don't need you getting all sloppy on me. Okay?"

It was a fair enough request. He'd downed three generously-filled glasses of Knob Creek in the time between Lily's departure and Nora's arrival. Another couple glasses and he would be stepping firmly into the territory of the sloppily drunk, no doubt.

He nodded. "Be right back."

He returned a few minutes later with Nora's drink. She took a long sip from it before setting the glass on the coffee table. She then shifted around on the sofa to face Johnny more directly, tucking her legs beneath her. Her hair was up and she was still clad in business attire—a black skirt, a grey blouse, and black stockings. Her two-inch heels were on the floor. The way her legs looked in those stockings filled Johnny's head with some vividly erotic ideas, some of which he hoped might become reality a little later.

"So…are we sure we know what Lily really meant when she said she knew you were there yesterday?"

Johnny rubbed at his eyes. "I don't see how it could be about anything other than me being at her place."

Nora frowned. "But you told me yesterday she was passed out drunk."

Johnny nodded. "That's right. At least I thought she was. Maybe she was faking. Maybe she knew I was there the whole time."

"But *how?*"

"I don't *know*, okay? I'm just guessing. And for the record, I don't actually believe she was faking. I know a genuine dead-to-the-world drunk when I see one, but…"

Johnny frowned as he trailed off, snatches of memory from the previous day replaying in his head.

Nora prompted him. "But?"

"But I made some noise on the way out of there. A car was pulling up outside. Remember? I told you about that. Anyway, I sort of collided with the table in the kitchen in my hurry to get out. Some bottles rolled off and broke on the floor. Maybe the noise woke her up and she was able to get to the kitchen in time to see me running across the back yard."

Nora grimaced. "Fuck."

Johnny grunted. "I know."

"*Fuck.*" Nora reached for her drink and gulped down most of it. Her emphatic tone and the bleak look on her face mirrored Johnny's own feelings on the subject. "That has to be what happened. Don't you think?"

Johnny nodded. "I can't think of any other plausible way she could know. A neighbor could have spotted me, but I sort of doubt that. And anyway, a neighbor wouldn't have known who I was. Unless she saw me with her own eyes, she'd never have known I was there. I'm sure about that, if nothing else."

Nora's expression turned openly fearful for the first time. "Christ. Okay, so let's say she *did* see you. Do you think she's told the others yet? What if they come after you? Maybe it's time you went to the police."

Johnny frowned. "Going to the cops is a last resort. I don't need the aggravation and I could even get in some trouble myself. Last night you seemed to think it might be best if I walked away from the whole situation. Just washed my hands of it. Remember?"

"That was when I thought you'd gotten away clean. The whole dynamic of the thing has changed. Reaching out to the cops might complicate your life some, but at least you'd be safer once they start looking into it all." She tilted her head, giving him a funny look. "Unless there's more to your reluctance than you're letting on."

"What do you mean?"

Nora finished her drink and set the empty glass down. She fixed Johnny with a gaze so steely calm it made him want to look away, though he managed not to do that. "The whole reason you're in this mess to start with is your blindness when it comes to all things Lily. Just yesterday you were doing the whole white knight thing and look where it got you."

"That's not fair."

"The hell it isn't." Her tone was less than friendly now, verging on hostile. "Jesus, Johnny, some part of you is still clinging to the idea of protecting that bitch. That's the real reason you won't go to the police. You're willing to risk your own safety to keep her out of trouble."

"Bullshit."

Nora sniffed disdainfully. "Oh, yeah? Convince me otherwise."

Johnny had an angry retort he bit back because he didn't want the dispute blowing up into something bigger. He didn't want to risk fouling things up with Nora so soon into whatever was happening between them. So he gritted his teeth and forced himself to look at things from her point of view. She had more than sufficient cause to harbor doubts.

"I get why you're mad and why you'd see things that way. But after today all that shit with Lily is out the window. I may have been blind in the past, but not anymore. I truly have no desire to shield her from anything."

Nora gave him another of her appraising looks. Something in the way her features shifted a moment later made his knotted-up stomach unclench a little. "Well, that's great, Johnny. I'm pleased to hear it. So tell me again why you won't go to the police."

Johnny sighed.

He desperately wanted a drink.

"It's like I've already told you. I don't want the hassle. Besides, I'm almost positive she hasn't told her friends I was there."

"And why is that?"

"She knows if she told them they'd immediately want to get rid of me and she doesn't want that. Not because she has still has feelings for me—I know she doesn't—but because she needs money."

Nora responded with a slow nod. "And as long as you're around, she figures she can keep squeezing you for more of it, regardless of what you told her today."

"Probably."

"All right, so maybe you're safe for the time being, but what about in the longer term? It's hard to predict the behavior of people like Lily. She might have every intention of keeping your secret right now, but what if she gets too drunk one night and just lets it slip?"

Johnny frowned.

He had to admit he hadn't given that angle of it much thought. It troubled him.

"Huh."

Nora seemed equally disturbed by the notion and they sat there together in a deep, thoughtful silence for several minutes. The only sounds were the hum of the central A/C and the chiming of the grandfather clock in the foyer as it marked the arrival of six p.m.

Nora spoke when the clock finished chiming. "Johnny?"

There was something tentative in her tone, a strange hint of fearfulness intermingling with a burgeoning excitement.

Johnny arched an eyebrow. "Yes?"

Nora scooted a little closer to him and put a hand on his leg. The physical contact sent a pleasurable shiver through his body. There was a growing intensity in her gaze as she said, "What if we kill them?"

Johnny laughed. "Right."

"I'm serious."

Johnny looked at her, studied her expression.

She wasn't playing with him.

Johnny's grin froze on his face and he said nothing for long moments. He finally dragged a hand over his face to smooth out his features, the physical effort made necessary by his deep state of shock and disbelief. "That seems…maybe a little extreme."

Nora sneered. "Is it? You've made it clear you won't get the authorities involved. And you know what you're facing. The way I see it, it's you or them."

Johnny searched her face for signs that this was some kind of sick joke on her part, after all. He saw nothing of the sort. Maybe she had a better poker face than most people— *probably* she did—but in this case he was sure she meant what she was saying.

He abruptly rose from the couch. "I'll need to fortify my nerves before we can continue this line of discussion."

Nora regarded him with an even expression and said nothing.

Johnny went into the kitchen and poured himself a tall glass of whiskey. While he was in there, he allowed himself a moment of silent freaking out. He fell back against the edge of the kitchen counter and put a hand to his chest to feel the rapid, stuttering beat of his heart.

Nora's proposal of murder had his head swirling with a riot of confusing and conflicting thoughts and ideas. He had expected nothing from her but intelligent, rational, and, most of all, *calm* opinions on how to deal with his problem. The reality that she had almost immediately embraced the most extreme option of all was, to say the least, disconcerting.

He hadn't the first clue how to respond.

He didn't even really want to go back into the living room.

Unfortunately, that wasn't a realistic option.

So Johnny grabbed his drink, took a big gulp from it, topped it off again, and rejoined Nora in the living room. To her credit, she gave him no grief about the drink, not even in the form of a sigh or cutting expression. That was something to be grateful for, at least.

He sat next to her and had another large gulp of Knob Creek. "Look...I know you said you were serious, but there's no way I'm committing triple goddamn homicide just to get my hapless ass out of a jam. Let's just be clear about that right now."

"You wouldn't have to do it alone. I'd help you."

Johnny gaped at her. "You're kidding."

Nora shook her head. "Not at all."

"Why in fuck would you do that?"

"Because I like you."

Johnny laughed. "Shit, I like you, too. But I can't see going on a killing spree on your behalf so early in the relationship."

There was a touch of heat in Nora's voice when she spoke again, the careful neutrality she'd maintained over the previous several minutes crumbling in the face of Johnny's flat dismissal of her idea. "So what's your plan then, Johnny? You mean to just sit back and make the most of whatever time you've got left until they come for you?"

"We don't even know for sure that'd happen. It's just guesswork."

"Some pretty damn educated guesswork, I'd say." Nora snatched her purse off the coffee table and got to her feet. "I'll be going now, Johnny. It's been lovely knowing you."

"Whoa. Hold on." Johnny sent a bit of his drink sloshing over the rim of the glass in his haste to get up. He set the glass on the coffee table and took Nora gently by an arm, sensing she wanted him to convince her to stay. Otherwise she would have been out the door already. In his experience, no one moved more quickly than a woman with a genuine desire to get away from a man. "Come on, we can talk about this some more. Lay out your case for this. I promise I'll listen with an open mind."

Nora sniffed. "So far your record where promises are concerned is shaky."

Johnny nodded. "I know. I promise I'll do better."

Nora laughed and shook her head.

But she sat back down.

Johnny heaved a relieved breath and sat next to her. He picked up his drink and downed more than half of it in a single pull. "All right, go on, make your case."

Nora started talking.

She didn't stop talking for at least fifteen minutes. A lot of it was reiteration of everything she'd already said but stated more emphatically and couched in terms that brooked no dissent. She also explained at length how her solution was actually the most logical and sensible way to go, given his stated desire to stay alive and his refusal to involve the police. Killing them all would eliminate Lily's implied threat of exposure and avoid entirely the potential of eventually being targeted by Bree and Slick. At its core, the idea was simple, but Nora's presentation was effusively dramatic and included numerous tangents relating to ancillary issues.

By the time she finished, Johnny was half-convinced she was right. He still had no intention of going through with it, but he could see the sense in it. The problem was he couldn't imagine himself committing acts of cold-blooded murder, even in the interest of self-protection. However, he chose not to share this conviction with Nora for the time being, at least until he could come up with a good way of putting her off the idea.

"All right, you've made a solid case, I'll admit that." He sighed. "But, look, I can't rush into a decision on this one way or another. It's a big fucking leap to take, killing three people, and I need some time to think it over."

Nora had been watching him in an intent, deadly serious way that was more than a little unnerving. Johnny knew she was gauging his reaction carefully and was trying to decide whether to believe him. He had a feeling it was touch and go there for a few moments, but finally the corners of her mouth curved upward in a small smile. "Okay. You think about it, Johnny. I'm sure in the end you'll see I'm right." She leaned close and put her hand on his leg again. "But be careful not to think too long. If you drag your heels on this long enough, the bad guys might act first."

Johnny didn't know what to say to that, mostly because it seemed to him that the line between who was a "bad" guy and who wasn't had blurred considerably.

He touched Nora's hand and leaned closer to her, close enough that their lips were almost touching. Her smile brightened at the shift toward intimacy and a distinctly lascivious twinkle appeared in her eyes. "You're right, I know you are, but do you think we could maybe forget about it a while and focus on other things?" His hand went to one of her stocking-covered legs and caressed it. "More pleasant things, like seeing you naked."

She laughed softly and kissed him teasingly on the mouth. Then she put her arms around his neck and said, "Now that you mention it, I think we could both use the distraction."

They kissed again, more hungrily this time.

In a while, they retired to Johnny's master bedroom and made love that was initially gentle and exquisitely precise but which soon turned frenzied and animalistic.

Per Johnny's ardent request, Nora left the stockings on.

14

Per his usual habit, Johnny drove out to the square the next day, but not until after the locksmith he'd contacted came by for the scheduled morning appointment. The man had the locks switched out by noon. The rush job meant his final fee was inflated by an obscene percentage, but Johnny didn't care much. He was just glad to have it done.

It was noon by the time he parked in his usual spot outside the Delirium Lounge. By then he was already itching for a drink. He didn't want to get loaded too soon and decided to take a leisurely stroll around the square.

A roundabout shepherded a steady stream of traffic around the area as the lunch hour lengthened. The traffic never moved too quickly, though, and pedestrians regularly ambled from one side of the street to the other, many of whom were either coming from or en route to the courthouse in the middle of the square. A pre-Civil War building, the courthouse had a clock tower that was one of the city's best-known landmarks.

As he walked, Johnny exchanged friendly smiles and nods with regulars in the area he'd come to know during his months of unemployment. He stopped for brief chats with a few of them. Occasionally he ducked into a shop to escape the heat and do a bit of browsing. More than once he saw things he thought he might buy for Nora, but he refrained because he wasn't sure he knew her tastes well enough yet. At Little Shop of Records he dropped in to talk music with Grant, the proprietor, and pre-ordered some new releases on vinyl.

His tour of the square concluded back at the Delirium Lounge. It had been a pleasant diversion, a way of taking his mind off some of the dire shit bearing down on him. He liked Nora, but he was having difficulty reconciling his interest in her with her coldly pragmatic attitude regarding murder. It disturbed him and hinted at an inner darkness that could be suggestive of other troublesome issues. How much could you really trust someone who was that unemotional about the prospect of killing people? Did this mean she was a sociopath? Or a psychopath?

Or whatever?

Johnny made a mental note—look up the exact definitions of those fucking words before the end of the day.

Meanwhile, drink.

A young girl wearing cateye-style glasses was behind the bar. Johnny figured her for a student. She was slender and pretty and had kind of a naughty librarian vibe happening, with the glasses and the way she wore her hair up. It was a look Johnny found irresistibly appealing. She also had numerous tattoos, which made him think of the dead girl and Lily. These were unwelcome thoughts. He wanted to push all that stuff away for as long as he could. The girl smiled when she saw him staring at her.

"Hey, Johnny."

"Hey…"

I can't remember your fucking name, please help me out here.

She laughed. "It's Riley. I just started here a few days ago. You were kind of, ah, tipsy my first day on the job."

Johnny nodded. "I sometimes resemble that description."

Riley laughed again. "What can I get you?"

What Johnny really wanted was a double whiskey, four of them lined up on the bar right in front of him. For starters.

What he said was, "A beer. Yazoo Hop Project."

She put a pint glass under the tap and began to fill it.

Johnny glanced at the television. No ballgame on yet, just some crazy damn thing on the Cartoon Network featuring a talking bird and his squirrel buddy. He looked at Riley. She'd nearly finished pulling his pint. "Riley's a damn odd name for a girl."

She smirked. "Maybe so. But it's a lot more creative than 'Johnny', wouldn't you say?"

Johnny grunted. "You got me there, doll."

Riley put a napkin in front of him and set the pint glass on that.

Johnny lifted the pint glass and sprinkled some salt from a shaker on the napkin.

Riley frowned. "What's up with that?"

Johnny sipped beer and wiped his mouth with the back of a hand. "Keeps the glass from sticking to the napkin. Watch."

He demonstrated.

Riley smiled. "You got any more tricks up your sleeve?"

"Tons. You wouldn't believe how many."

Riley leaned against the bar, braced her elbows on its edge, and framed her pretty face in her upraised palms. She was very close. "Well, you'll have to teach me some more of them."

Johnny looked at her, his brow furrowing.

Huh.

"How old are you?"

She looked right at him and said, "Old enough."

"Huh."

Jesus. I'm getting hit on all over the place all of a sudden. What is this, backwards week?

"Is this backwards week?"

She laughed and pushed back from the bar. "I don't think so, but hey, the place *is* called the Delirium Lounge, 'delirium' being a word implying a deranged state of mind, so maybe you have to be a little off-kilter to work or drink here. Who's to say, really? It's a goddamn mystery."

Johnny sighed. In another life, he would have been instantly, hopelessly obsessed with this girl. But she was maybe half his age and that life was long gone.

Riley frowned and shook her head. "Jesus. You look like a guy in a war movie who knows he's seconds away from being gunned down on Omaha Beach or some shit." She laughed and waved a hand at the bar's entrance. "Take a look out there. It's a beautiful day. The sun is shining, laughter is in the air. Okay, so I can't actually hear the laughter, but I know it's out there. Be happy, Johnny. Life is good."

Johnny forced a weary smile. He raised his pint glass and tipped it at her. "Right. Here's to happiness."

One day she would be old enough to realize true happiness didn't exist, except as a fleeting illusion you were sometimes allowed on the road to more misery. But she was young and deserved to be humored on that count.

Riley's expression abruptly sobered. "Oh, shit. You're not terminal or something, are you? If you are, I'm really fucking sorry."

"Um…no."

Though someone out there may terminate me soon if I'm not careful.

"Phew." Riley's face registered obvious relief. "Thought I'd made an ass of myself there for a second."

Johnny chuckled. "No worries, Riley. Never apologize for being an optimist."

The front door swung open and a man who had the look of a slick 80's lawyer or Wall Street exec came into the bar. He had an overabundance of product in his hair and wore red suspenders over a shirt and tie. The shirt was powder blue with a crisp white collar. Johnny didn't know the guy, but decided to think of him as Gordon. As in Gordon Gekko from *Wall Street*, Oliver Stone's iconic film about 80's greed and excess. The only thing off was the color of the suspenders. Gordon moseyed up to the bar and settled his narrow ass on a stool five down from where Johnny sat.

Johnny and Riley exchanged a look that communicated a shared amusement. Riley put a hand over her mouth to stifle laughter. Johnny was smiling as she moved away to serve the newcomer. Gosh, she was a really swell gal. He wished like hell he could invent some kind of age reversal potion. He imagined being able to shave off twenty years simply by dropping a tablet in his beer. That'd be a neat trick. Not only would he feel less guilty about flirting with the cute young barmaid, he'd become rich in the bargain. The world was overflowing with out-of-shape middle-aged guys facing similar dilemmas. He could become the goddamn Donald Trump of age manipulation and retire to fucking Tahiti within a year.

Johnny was feeling a bit loopy.

He stared at his half-empty pint glass and wondered whether he'd somehow lost track and had ten beers instead of just two.

No.

That didn't seem likely. His odd mood was probably just a side-effect of exposure to the enchanting Riley. His mood sobered some when a folded-over newspaper someone had left on the bar snagged his attention. He might have ignored it, but something he caught a partial glimpse of caused him to drag the paper over and flip it open. His gut clenched when he saw the lead story and got a full look at the picture he'd glimpsed. It showed an attractive young woman, probably in her early twenties, with long black hair and a gorgeous, high-wattage smile. The bold headline to the left of the picture read, MTSU STUDENT MISSING.

Oh, shit.

Something in Johnny screamed at him not to read the story, but he ignored the impulse and read it anyway, though he did so with a continually mounting sense of dread and impending doom. He initially clung to a fragile hope that the woman in the story and the dead woman he'd seen in Lily's duplex were not the same person, but by the time he'd finished the story's third paragraph he was certain they were. She had been missing for exactly two days, for one thing, but the clincher was the description of her "distinctive" tattoos. The girl's name was Jamie Benton and she'd last been seen leaving a bar in the early morning hours in nearby Nashville in the company of a trio of unidentified companions, two females and one male.

Johnny grimaced at this detail.

Slick, Bree, and Lily. No doubt about it. Shit.

Jamie Benton had only been twenty-two-years-old.

Johnny stared at her picture and wondered how many hearts had been set aflutter by that lovely smile during her twenty-two years. Too many to count, probably. But her beauty had been erased from the world forever. And now he was being forced to again confront a thing that had been bothering him all along—the idea that there would be no justice for this once-vibrant girl and no closure for her family.

All because he was concerned first and foremost with his own interests. And because he didn't want to endure the bother of an investigation. Johnny stared at the dead girl's picture and felt his chest tighten. He couldn't breathe and the walls around him felt too close

Gotta get out of here, get some fucking air.

Feeling numb, he dragged his wallet out after sliding off his stool. Riley had just wandered back over and was staring at him with obvious concern as he threw too many bills on the bar. Her mouth opened and she said something, but it was just noise to Johnny as he turned away from her and staggered out of the Delirium Lounge.

15

The sun felt too bright as the bar's door whispered shut behind him. Johnny wished for sunglasses and tried to remember if he had a pair stashed away somewhere in the Austin-Healey. Probably. He opened the car's passenger side door and leaned in to flip open the glove box. He shivered with relief as he spied the dark sunglasses and had just closed a hand around them when he felt something press into his back.

His heart lurched.

It felt like the barrel of a gun.

"That's exactly what you think it is."

Johnny went rigid at the sound of that voice. He had last heard it while hiding in a closet and listening to two psychos talking about what to do with a dead body. One of the psychos had apparently come to kill him. Though he had known this was a possibility, he hadn't expected it to happen this soon. He was astonished Lily hadn't kept the information about his presence at the scene to herself at least a little longer. Thinking she would do so to have something to hold over his head had been a reasonable assumption.

Or perhaps he was just a hopelessly naïve jackass.

Slick Hogan said, "We're gonna go for a ride, Johnny. When I step back, you won't see the gun, but it's gonna be aimed right at your anyway, I promise you that. You're gonna be calm as shit, the totally chill Johnny Doyle everybody knows. You're gonna act like you're happy to see your old pal Slick. And then we're both getting in this sweet ride of yours."

Johnny swallowed and said, "And what happens then?"

His heart was pounding and his mouth felt uncomfortably dry. A sheen of sweat formed on his forehead and the sensation of experiencing everything a little too intensely that had driven him out of the Delirium Lounge returned in full force. He felt like he might either throw up or drop dead on the spot, because he thought he knew the real answer to his question. Slick would lie about it, but Johnny would hear the truth of it in his voice.

"We're going to your house, Johnny."

Johnny frowned. It wasn't what he'd expected to hear. "What? Why?"

Slick pressed the gun a little harder against his back. "We'll get to that later. I'm stepping back now. You do what I fucking said."

The pressure of the gun barrel against his back went away and Johnny let out a breath. He listened to the frantic hammering of his heart a moment before backing out of the Austin-Healey and turning around to face his adversary. The sunglasses were clutched in his right hand. He hooked them over the collar of his Hawaiian shirt and beamed at Slick in a way passersby might well have taken for genuine happy surprise.

"You're not gonna shoot me in broad daylight in a public place, Slick. Even you're not that stupid."

Slick's right hand was shoved deep inside the pocket of a leather motorcycle jacket, which he was wearing open over a white wife-beater shirt. A bulge in the pocket was aimed right at Johnny's abdomen. The former white gangsta thug turned 50's-style greaser smirked in a way that made him look like a deranged Elvis Presley. "You're right about that, Johnny. You're a real smart guy. But here's the thing. You remember Bree, right? She's that stone crazy chick I was jawing with while you were cowering like a pussy in the closet. Well, right now she's in the parking lot outside a SouthTrust bank, where a pretty little loan officer I hear you've been boning should be returning from her lunch hour soon."

Johnny's face hardened. "The fuck are you saying, asshole?"

Slick went right on smirking. "I think you know what I'm saying. If Bree doesn't hear the right news from me in the next few minutes, pretty Nora's brains are gonna get splattered all over that parking lot." His smirk became an aggressive leer. "You got any more smartass bullshit to say to me or are we going for that ride?"

Johnny's shoulders sagged in defeat. "Get in, goddammit. You call Bree as soon as we're in the car, you hear me? Otherwise we're not going anywhere."

Slick chuckled. "I hear you, pops. Let's get this show on the road."

They got in the car.

Slick made the call.

After heaving a big sigh of relief, Johnny got the car started and drove away from the Delirium Lounge.

16

They pulled into the driveway at Johnny's house just under fifteen minutes later. During the drive, Johnny was able to squeeze a few pertinent facts out of a smug Slick Hogan, who was all-too-willing to spell out for him the events leading up to Johnny's imminent demise.

Much of it was what Johnny would have guessed. Lily got drunk and spilled the beans. Slick and Bree freaked out. Both wanted to head over to Johnny's house and put a bullet in his head immediately. Lily was down with that, but she talked them into waiting until the next day. She told them Johnny had a new squeeze. She didn't know who it was, but she was sure they could squeeze a significant cash payment out of Johnny by threatening the bitch. All they had to do was find out the mystery woman's identity, which Lily was able to do in short order early the next morning by reconnecting with certain gossipy elements of their former shared social circle.

Johnny looked at Slick after shutting off the car. "You've gotta promise me one thing."

Slick laughed. "Way I see it, you're in no position to demand anything. But hey, I'm a generous guy. Ask anybody. What's your last request, old man?"

Johnny leveled a steady, unflinching gaze at him. "I'm done for, I know that, but you have to leave Nora alone. She doesn't know anything about what you fuckers did."

Slick snickered. "You expect me to believe that?"

"It's the truth."

Slick peered at him closely, straining to see the lie behind Johnny's unwavering mask of faux-sincerity. Then he grinned. "You know what, old-timer? You've got my word. So long as your story checks out, nothing will happen to Nora. There. You happy?"

"What do you mean if my story checks out?"

Slick laughed. "Come on, Johnny. You don't expect me to take your word for it, do you? I'll have a little talk with her and get a feel for what she knows. If I don't get the wrong kind of vibe from her, she gets to keep on living. Okay?"

Johnny sighed.

This could be nothing more than Slick telling him what he wanted to hear in order to speed things along to the next phase of the farce in which the two of them were engaged. Killing Nora might well be the next item on the hoodlum's to-do list, something he'd take care of as soon as his business with Johnny was concluded. Hell, it was more of a probability than a possibility. Still, despite the dubious nature of the "promise" he'd extracted from Slick, Johnny knew it was the best he could hope for given the circumstances.

"Good enough." Johnny stared at his house a moment before glancing at Slick. "So what's next?"

"This is your place, right?"

"It ain't the fucking White House."

Slick tossed his head back and laughed heartily at that one. The exaggerated belly-laugh went on long enough to make Johnny's skin crawl. Slick was a different animal from your standard-issue thug. While he wasn't as overtly unhinged as Bree Sloan, there was something off about him. For Slick, this wasn't about anything as simple as parting a man from his money. This was a guy who enjoyed toying with people and instilling terror.

It was a game for him.

It was *fun*.

For the first time in his life, Johnny actively wanted to kill another human being. And Slick saw it. This was evident in the way the big, phony grin froze on his face and slowly wilted away to a dour glare.

"Fun time's over. Out of the car, dead meat."

Johnny didn't bother with a retort, having revealed enough truth with that one look of open hostility. From here on out—until this stupid thug fired a bullet through his head—he would have to swallow his anger and pride and be nothing but servile. He was close to certain Slick had no intention of sparing Nora. On the off-chance Johnny was wrong about that, however, he had no choice but to go to his grave like a whipped dog.

As Slick followed him down the sidewalk toward the porch, Johnny kept his head in a rigid, locked position, giving an impression of being focused on nothing other than entering his house. However, he was surreptitiously searching the surrounding area in hopes of catching the eye of a nosy neighbor, someone who knew him well enough to guess something was amiss. But the street was empty and none of the neighbors were outside tending to their yards.

Where the hell is everybody?

But then the answer came to him. This was the time of day when gainfully employed people were at their jobs. Though he'd only been out of work a relatively short while, it seemed longer somehow, as if the whole professional phase of his life had been nothing more than some kind of illusion or fever dream. Some of that had to do with the drinking, but he thought more of it was that, for him, there'd never been much of a correlation between the work he did and who he really was. Lots of people lived and breathed their jobs. They worked long hours and when they were away from the office it was still at the center of everything. It was all they talked about with their spouses when they got home or with their pals—almost always co-workers—over beers at whatever local watering hole they favored.

He had almost forgotten it was like that for so many people.

For Johnny, not working felt natural. If he could come up with some way of making his money last, he thought he could happily go on being a perpetually soused and unemployed gadabout for the rest of his life. Now, of course, it looked like the question of how long he might sustain that lifestyle was about to become a non-issue.

Johnny climbed the steps to his porch and jabbed his house key at the lock. It slid into the slot maybe a quarter inch before meeting resistance.

He frowned and tried again.

Same result.

The fuck?

"There a problem?"

Johnny flinched at Slick's voice, which was closer than expected. He could feel the asshole's breath against the side of his neck. He cast a glance over his shoulder. "Will you please back off and let me figure this shit out?"

Slick slid the gun out of his pocket and aimed it at Johnny's back, using his body to shield it from the view of anyone who might happen by. "You just get that door open, son, or I'll shoot you dead right here and take off in your car."

Johnny tried hard not to show his fear. "Just give me a minute, okay?"

Slick winked and moved back a small step.

Johnny let out a breath and focused again on getting the door open. The key again failed to slide easily into the slot. He tried jamming it in with greater force for a moment before abandoning the effort as obviously futile. He stared at the key in dumbstruck frustration for a long moment, knowing damn well this was the same key he'd used to enter this house for the last decade.

Then he remembered.

"Oh, for fuck's sake."

Slick grunted. "What now?"

In his terror, Johnny had forgotten about the locksmith's morning visit. The new house key was attached to the thick key

ring by a little twist of wire. Silently cursing his obviously failing short-term memory, he slid the new key into the lock and
turned it.

Slick chuckled and pressed the gun against his back.
"Just in the nick of time."

Johnny said nothing and entered the house.

Slick followed him inside and kicked the door shut behind him. The door slammed into the frame hard enough to
rattle the grandfather clock in the living room—visible through a
wide archway to the left—and set off a series of discordant
chimes. "All right, Johnny, where's the safe?"

Johnny tugged a cigarillo out of his breast pocket and
wedged it into a corner of his mouth, smirking around it as he lit
up with his Zippo. "So that's what this is about."

Slick nodded. "Lily saw it when she was here. Said it
had to be new."

So his ex-wife had done serious snooping around before
he'd walked in on her. The revelation gave him new cause to
regret his former open-door policy. Good thing the safe was
such a hefty block of solid steel, otherwise she might have
walked off with it. Not that it mattered now.

Johnny exhaled smoke. "How about I give you all the
money in it and we put an end to this without bloodshed. You
must have figured out I've got no interest in telling the cops anything."

"I believe you, but it doesn't matter." A hint of something that might have been regret briefly flickered in Slick's
eyes. "As long as you're breathing, there'll always be that
chance you might change your mind and I can't risk that."

Johnny nodded. "About what I figured. Had to ask."

He blew a stream of smoke straight at Slick's face.

Slick waved the smoke away and glowered at Johnny.
"Do that again, cocksucker, and I'll put the fucking thing out in
your eye."

Johnny smiled. "Duly noted. Safe's this way."

He turned away from Slick and continued through the large foyer toward the hallway entrance straight ahead. His heart was thudding hard. The knowledge that he might be in the last few minutes of his life made him unsteady on his feet. He regretted antagonizing Slick. On a rational level, Johnny knew the smoke thing made no real difference one way or another. Slick's course had been set from the beginning. This was just that desperate-to-survive part of his psyche making noise. It was a voice he suspected would only get louder as the final moments ticked away. Any second now he would start weeping and begging for his life. The prospect repelled him, but he knew instinct would override pride.

Slick whistled as they continued making their way through the house. "Nice digs, man. Gotta hand it to you. For such an asshole, you really knew how to live in style."

Johnny said nothing and puffed on his cigarillo.

Slick laughed. "Really getting scared now, huh?"

They reached the open door to his office. Johnny stepped through it and turned on the light. That desperate-to-survive part of his psyche was screaming at him, practically begging him to think of delaying tactics. Something, anything at all, to forestall the inevitable even a little bit longer. But he ignored the useless impulse and headed straight for the safe.

Slick laughed in that irritatingly insidious way of his as he came into the office. "You know, it's funny. You've got this nice house and all this money, but you're really not so smart."

The safe was on a bookshelf at roughly eye-level. Johnny's side was turned toward Slick as he began to spin the combination dial. "Oh, yeah? How do you figure?"

Slick looked smugger than ever now. "Because you're so damn slow to catch on."

Johnny frowned and paused with his hand on the dial. "The fuck are you talking about?"

Slick grinned big. He looked full of himself, as pleased as a mischievous child who's just pulled a big one over on his parents. But now he was spilling all because he wanted Johnny to know how incredibly clever he had been. "You got played. And it was *easy*, man, fucking *easy*."

Johnny took the cigarillo out of his mouth and turned in Slick's direction. "All right, I got played. How?"

"Bree ain't really in on this deal."

Johnny stared at Slick in silent incomprehension for a long moment.

And then it hit him.

"Oh, for fuck's sake."

Slick nodded. "Your girl was never in danger. Might be later, who knows, but today? Nah. Bree doesn't even know about you. If she did, you'd both be dead already."

"That call you made…"

"Lilly. Playing along just like she was supposed to."

Johnny sighed.

Slick filled in the rest. Part of his original story had been true. Lily got drunk and blabbed everything. But Bree hadn't been within earshot at the time and Slick had convinced her to keep it between the two of them. There was money to be made and a two-way split of the pie was a sweeter deal than divvying it up three ways. Though he didn't say it outright, Johnny guessed Slick meant to get rid of Bree soon. Maybe it was hard feelings over her taking that shot at him. Maybe it was something else. Who the hell knew?

"So tell me, Johnny—how smart do you feel right now?"

Johnny sighed and rested his forehead against the edge of a bookshelf. "Not very smart."

Slick's laughter was cold and heartless. "Get the goddamn safe open. *Now.*"

Johnny dropped the cigarillo in an ashtray on his desk. He gave the safe's dial a twist and started the combination from the beginning. There was nothing left now but to meet his fate with what little dignity he could manage. A few more rapid twists of the dial and the safe's door came open.

His eyes widened as he pulled the door fully open and looked inside. "Huh."

"What?" Slick sounded impatient. "Something wrong?"

Johnny shook his head. "No."

"Then what the fuck? There's money in there, right?"

"There's more than I remembered."

"Well, get it out then," Slick said, sounding exasperated.

Johnny nodded. "Yeah. Okay."

He reached inside the safe and curled his fingers around the grip of the 9mm pistol. After thumbing the safety to the off position, he stepped back and turned on Slick, leveling the gun on him in a motion so smooth and fluid it would have been the envy of anyone with training in police tactics. He aimed for center mass and squeezed off a shot before Slick could even begin to react. He shifted his aim and fired again a millisecond later.

The first bullet took Slick in the chest, crimson instantly staining his white wife-beater shirt. His stupefied expression conveyed shock and terror.

Then the second bullet wiped the look off his face.

17

The sound of the doorbell jerked Johnny out of a daze. About a half hour had passed since he'd put two rounds through Slick Hogan and ended his life. He still couldn't believe he'd killed another human being. Thirty minutes wasn't nearly long enough to process the psychological ramifications of what he'd done. Give him thirty *years* and maybe he could begin to come to terms with it.

Maybe.

Ice cubes rattled as Johnny downed the rest of his second whiskey.

But not likely.

The whiskey was to help settle his stomach. After shooting Slick, he became violently ill and ran out of his office. His destination had been the nearest bathroom, but he only made it to the hallway outside the office when his stomach abruptly decided it couldn't wait and ejected its contents right then and there.

There were still vast puddles of vomit on the hallway's hardwood floor. He hadn't yet mustered the energy necessary to clean it up. Just the thought of venturing in that direction again sent shivers of dread through his body.. It would all have to be dealt with at some point—the body *and* the mess—but a good bit more whiskey might be necessary first.

The doorbell rang again.

In fact, it had been ringing insistently for several moments. Someone out there on the porch was repeatedly jabbing at the button with maniacal intensity. Whoever it was desperately wanted inside his house. Given what had transpired, it was hard to take that as anything other than a very bad sign.

But then he heard a muffled voice calling out to him from the other side of the door.

Johnny frowned.

That sounds like…oh…yeah…

After he'd finally managed to drag himself out of the puke-splattered hallway, some dim instinct made him reach out to Nora, the only person he could trust under the circumstances. His recollection of this was foggy. He had barely been coherent during the brief phone conversation. But now she was here, no doubt in a state of blind panic after listening to Johnny's mumbled rantings about murder and blood.

Johnny heaved himself off the sofa with a groan and staggered off in the direction of the foyer. By some miracle he got to the door without falling over. He hauled it open and Nora took one cringing look at him before barging her way inside. After shutting the door and turning the lock, she took hold of Johnny by an arm and steered him back to the living room. She maintained her grip on him until he was safely settled on the sofa again.

Then she stood over him with her hands on her hips and regarded him with considerable concern. "All right, Johnny, what's going on? The sooner I know what's happened, the sooner I can start fixing it."

"My mess." Johnny slurred his words slightly, as if he'd had too much to drink. The real reason was disorientation caused by severe psychological trauma. He wondered dimly whether Nora could tell the difference. "Fixing it's…my job…"

"Right now you'd have trouble fixing yourself a sandwich. So stop with the nonsense and…" Nora frowned as she trailed off, lifting her chin and cocking her head to one side. She sniffed at the air and grimaced. "Oh, God, what is that vile smell?"

Johnny made a vague gesture. "An array of things. Vomit. Gunpowder. Possibly some fecal matter."

Nora squinted at him. "Fecal matter?"

Johnny shrugged. "I hear corpses sometimes void their bowels at the moment of death."

Nora groaned in sudden comprehension. "Stay right there."

"Yes, ma'am."

It was maybe the easiest to obey command he'd ever received.

Nora stalked out of the living room with a grim but determined look on her face, choosing to let her nose guide her to the putrid scent's source rather than asking Johnny where to look. Johnny stared at the empty glass on the coffee table and waited to hear her shriek of alarm.

But several minutes passed and there was no audible reaction from Nora. In a while, he heard her heels clicking on the hardwood floor again, but she didn't immediately return to the living room. He soon heard a rattle of glass and ice cubes from the kitchen, followed by the sloshing sound of liquid being poured out of a bottle.

Johnny couldn't help smiling.

In his estimation, a drink was an appropriate first response after your first up-close look at a bullet-riddled body.

Hell, it made for pretty solid second and third steps as well.

Nora returned to the living room with a vodka martini and bottles of Absolut and Knob Creek. She splashed a modest amount of whiskey into Johnny's glass before sitting next to him on the sofa. They sat and drank in contemplative silence for a few moments. Johnny finished off the bit of whiskey Nora had poured for him in short order and splashed in a little more. Nora's expression told him she wouldn't be pleased if he filled it to the brim. Given the situation, he saw the sense in moderation, so he made himself sip more slowly.

Nora spoke first.

"This is good."

Johnny gaped at her a moment before responding. Then he swallowed thickly and said, "What?"

Nora touched him lightly on the knee. "I mean it, Johnny. This is *good*. All you've done here is start us down the path I already knew we should take. Granted, it's not an *ideal* start. We've got a hell of a mess to clean up. But this is the right choice. I'm more sure of that now than ever."

Johnny winced as understanding dawned. She was talking about the startlingly bloodthirsty opinion she'd voiced last night—that they could solve Johnny's dilemma by killing all of them. He almost laughed.

One down, two to go.

The question of how to put Nora off the idea had consumed nearly the whole of his attention earlier in the day. But this was the first time he'd thought of it since his run-in with Slick. He still had no interest in killing anyone. He wished he hadn't had to kill Slick, but the sneering son of a bitch had given him no choice.

He was a killer. It was a simple fact of his existence and there could never be any taking it back. And now a dark voice at the back of his mind, one he was sure he'd never heard before, was saying maybe Nora was right. Maybe it was time to strike fast and kill the rest of them. Then—and only then—he might have some hope of putting this wretched business behind him.

He stomach knotted at the thought of it, an instinctive reaction that was a vestige of his lingering affection for Lily. No matter what happened, he couldn't seem to permanently divest himself of those old feelings. Though he thought this was to his credit—being an affirmation that some shred of his humanity was intact—another, less sentiment-driven part of his psyche recognized that it made him more of a chump than ever.

Lily had conspired with Slick.

Had marked him for death.

That same dark voice whispered something even more disturbing—that though he wasn't quite okay with it yet, it was possible he could *become* okay with the idea of killing his ex-wife.

He shuddered and ran a hand through his hair.

Nora squeezed his knee and smiled in sympathy. "I know this won't be easy on you. If you want, I can be the one to take care of Lily. It was my idea after all, so it's only fair I do my share. But before we can even start figuring out the rest of it, I need you to tell me exactly what happened here. Leave nothing out."

Johnny filled his glass again.

Took a deep drink.

And started talking.

18

Nora's idea about how to dispose of the body surprised Johnny. Most people with a body to get rid of tended to drive them way out to some remote spot in the country to dump them in a ravine or bury them in the woods. Burial seemed safer than a simple dumping. Unless you got caught in the act, it would reduce greatly the chances of eventual discovery of the remains. Johnny hadn't much relished the idea of the physical labor required—digging a grave big enough and deep enough to accommodate the late Slick Hogan would be a lot of sweaty, tiresome work—but he supposed one did whatever was necessary in these situations.

But Nora's suggestion eliminated the need for all that. And they would only have to transport the body to a location within the city limits. Of course, this was a prospect infinitely preferable to the dreary possibility of a trip out to the sticks. Another potentially huge upside was that there would be no remains left to discover.

Nora had a friend—more of an ardent admirer, actually—who was the proprietor of Miller Bros. Mortuary and Funeral Home.

Johnny slugged back an ounce or so of cold beer. He'd switched to it after finishing off that last big glass of Knob Creek. This time he had done it without a nudge from Nora, knowing damn well he couldn't afford to get hammered until this situation was resolved, regardless of how intensely he longed for the sweet, comforting embrace of deep inebriation.

He stifled a belch and looked at her. "This guy...you're sure you can trust him?"

A small smile dimpled the corners of her mouth. "He worships me, Johnny."

Johnny frowned and pulled at the edge of the bottle's glued-on paper label as he thought about that. A minimal amount of glue had been used and the label came away with ease. He had a flash of memory from his youth. It was said back then that if you could remove the label from a bottle of beer without tearing it, it was proof you were not a virgin. It was a kind of word-of-mouth meme from the days before the Internet. There was no sense in it, especially in light of the quite early loss of his virginity in middle school. He'd nonetheless always tried hard not to tear the labels when removing them. It was one of those little obsessions that had persisted down through the decades. He remembered the labels tearing at least half the time back in the day and was certain bottlers of beer used significant-ly less glue these days.

This was symptomatic of a larger problem in society, Johnny was sure.

Nobody had standards anymore.

Not even that noted lush Johnny Doyle, who apparently was on the verge of permanently flushing what remaining morals he had down the drain.

He held the label up for Nora to see. "Look, I'm not a virgin."

She stared blankly at it a moment before rolling her eyes. "Congratulations. That should impress all your buddies at the weekend kegger."

Johnny set the label on the coffee table. "How do you know this guy?"

Nora looked amused. "The Miller clan has been tight with my family for years and years. I got to know him at back-yard barbecues and the like. You sound jealous."

"Maybe. You hear someone else is interested in your girl, it gets your hackles up a little."

Nora arched an eyebrow. "Oh, so I'm your 'girl' now, am I?"

Johnny shrugged. "You're something, anyway. More than just a friend."

Nora laughed. "You won't be jealous once you get a look at Barry Miller. He's a bit of a toad. And that's being kind."

"I guess that's okay then."

Nora's features became slightly pinched. "I have no interest in Barry. But this is a big favor we'll be asking of him. I may have to do something for him."

Johnny didn't like the sound of that. "You're not gonna fuck him. Tell me you're not."

Nora gave her head an adamant shake. "I will not have intercourse with Barry the Toad. Not under any circumstances."

Johnny relaxed a little. "Oh, good."

"A blowjob, however, may be necessary."

Johnny groaned. "Jesus."

Nora plucked the half-empty beer bottle from his fingers and set it on the coffee table. She put her face close to his and snuggled against him. The physical contact produced the predictable stirring downstairs. He put his hand on her leg and stared into her eyes, the whites of which were utterly untouched by red, so unlike his own. She wasn't quite the bombshell Lily had been in her prime, but Nora's beauty was the kind that revealed itself more the longer one was in her presence. Every time he saw her a different aspect of it stood out to him in a new way. Her eyes were compelling, but now he found himself focusing on her mouth. The shape of it was exquisite. He was suddenly sure he had never seen lips quite so succulent.

He ached to kiss them.

But then he thought of those luscious lips wrapped around Barry Miller's cock.

He grimaced and shook his head. "Fuck."

She put a hand to his cheek. "Baby, be realistic. I don't like the idea, either. But a favor of this magnitude comes with a high price tag."

Johnny's laughter had a bitter tinge to it. "I guess you're right. Look, how do we really know he'll go for this? Okay, he's hot for you. I've got no problem believing that. Having a crush on a gorgeous babe is one thing, but doing highly illegal shit that could send his ass to fucking jail is something else altogether. You'll be taking a huge risk just by asking him about it. How confident are you in your ability to bend this guy to your will?"

The corners of Nora's mouth curved upward ever-so-slightly. "*Completely* confident."

Johnny held her gaze for a long moment.

Yes, it was a hell of a big risk. Maybe the biggest either of them had ever taken. But if it worked out, it would go a long ways toward permanently extricating them from this mess.

He kissed Nora on the mouth, tasting her lipstick and feeling that stirring again.

Then he broke off the kiss and said, "All right. Call the toad."

Nora grabbed her phone and retreated to a remote corner of Johnny's house to have her discussion with Barry Miller in private. She didn't emerge from the rarely used guest bedroom until nearly a half hour later, time enough for Johnny to put away a couple more cold beers, a pace that came close to negating the intent to stay clear-headed by avoiding the hard stuff. A person could get just as drunk off beer with only a little determination, a thing he knew but often forgot—until those times when he suddenly had a sea of empties in front of him and a vaguely recalled desire to take it easy for once.

Nora was visibly frustrated with him when she came back into the living room and saw the empties on the coffee table. "Jesus."

"What?"

She shook her head. "I've just spent a miserable eternity kissing the toad's ass. I was finally able to talk him into helping us, but it wasn't easy. And what have you been doing? You've been having a fucking party, that's what. I bet you haven't even started cleaning up in the office or thinking about how to get Slick out of here."

Johnny squirmed at her accusatory tone. He wanted to snap back at her, but there was a problem with that—she was right about all of it.

So he said the only thing he could: "I'm sorry."

Nora sighed. "You're done drinking until we've taken care of this." She moved closer to him and extended a hand. "Off your lazy ass, Johnny. We've got work to do."

This was another thing Johnny couldn't refute.

So they went to work.

Johnny broke out the cleaning supplies—including a mop and bucket—and they cleaned up the office and hallway. After that they wrapped Slick's body in multiple sets of bed sheets. That left the issue of which car to use for corpse transportation, the discussion of which eerily mirrored a similar debate Johnny had listened to while hiding in a closet recently, except that this time there was no gunplay.

By rights Johnny's car should have been used. He had killed Slick, so it should have been on him. But the Austin-Healey's trunk was too small and too crowded with too much old junk. After expressing some grumbling concerns about a possible future search of her car's trunk by corpse-sniffing dogs, Nora accepted reality and they used her car.

The iffy part was carrying the wrapped-up corpse out to the Mercedes. Johnny had a garage, but it too was crowded with junk. He had been using it for nothing but storage of random crap for several years. Excavating enough of it to make room for the Mercedes to pull in would have required hours of work, which was unacceptable.

They weighed their options and decided to take a big risk.

After verifying that the street was clear and that no one seemed to be in the vicinity, they dragged their heavy package out through Johnny's front door. A lot of huffing and puffing ensued as they worked to lift the package off the ground and wedge it into the trunk. By the time the deed was done, they were dripping with sweat. They leaned against the Mercedes and scanned the surrounding area for any indication that they'd been observed.

There was no such indication.

Nora wiped sweat from her brow. "I've got a dead guy in my car."

Johnny heaved a breath and took another look up and down the street. "Yeah."

"I never thought I'd have a dead guy in my car."

Johnny nodded. He really wanted a beer. "You can't anticipate a thing like that. Unless you're a mobster."

"Or a serial killer."

"Right. That, too."

Nora pushed away from the car and straightened her clothes. "Well, let's go get rid of him."

Johnny nodded again. He supported that idea one-hundred percent.

The sooner, the better.

They got in Nora's car and drove away from his house.

19

The toad wasn't so much of a toad, as it turned out. Oh, he wasn't handsome by any stretch, but Johnny's first glimpse of Barry Miller when he walked out of the mortuary's rear entrance confirmed what a piece of him had quietly suspected from the beginning, that Nora had exaggerated his hideousness.

Whereas Johnny packed the small bit of abdominal pudge typical of men his age, Barry was quite a bit rounder through the middle, despite being of the same approximate vintage. Add another ten pounds to him and he'd be straddling the line between an acceptable level of excess weight and actual obesity. Normally Johnny didn't like to judge people based on appearance, but in this case he felt justified in making an exception. He figured you were entitled to a little pettiness when the person in question was about to get his knob gobbled by your new girlfriend.

Also, he was balding. He had a smooth dome and a fringe of oily-looking black hair above his ears and at the back of his head. Johnny could never figure why guys like that didn't just go for the totally shorn look, which was a hell of a lot less goofy-looking. A certain kind of guy could make it look cool. Barry Miller wasn't that kind of guy. Not by a longshot. His shortcomings in that department made for quite the contrast to Johnny's lustrous blond locks.

Johnny watched Nora confer with Barry from the passenger seat of her Mercedes-Benz. The two of them were standing on the back stoop, which was shaded by a black awning that rippled gently in the wind. "M. Bros." was embossed across the awning's slanted top in dignified gold script. Barry wore the standard black attire of his profession. The two stood close together and spoke in whispers. The whispering Johnny understood. The subject matter being discussed warranted hushed voices. But he didn't much care for the close proximity. Nor did he much like it when Nora smiled and laughed in reaction to something the death merchant said. His clenching gut told him she liked Barry more than she'd let on. This was evident in the easy rapport the two enjoyed.

Johnny fidgeted and toyed with the idea of getting out of the car to have a word with them. His restlessness wasn't due only to the irritating display of friendliness between Nora and the funeral director, though that was certainly a significant part of it. The larger part of it was the knowledge of the gruesome cargo stashed in the trunk of the Mercedes.

Hopefully, there wouldn't be anything left to hide soon.

Unless, of course, Miller had come to his senses and was refusing to help them. That could be a valid reason for Nora's apparent amping up of the charm.

At long last, however, the conversation on the stoop concluded. Nora gave Miller's arm an apparently affectionate squeeze and came trotting back down the steps and across the asphalt toward the Mercedes. She opened the driver's side door and dropped in next to Johnny.

He tried hard not to sound overly cranky when he said, "That took a while."

Nora was still smiling as she peered through the windshield and waved at Miller, who was lingering on the stoop as he finished a cigarette. "We'll have to kill him later, you know."

Johnny's head swiveled slowly toward Nora. "What?"

"He's a loose end, Johnny."

Striving to keep his expression neutral, Johnny said, "Exactly how many more people are we supposed to kill before this fucking nightmare is over?"

"Exactly three more, if we do this quickly and cleanly and don't get anyone else involved." She cut her eyes at him, while managing to keep the smile in place. "We'll have the situation under control soon. There's no need to be melodramatic."

"But this guy's your friend, right? How can you be so cold about killing him?"

Nora said nothing for a moment, watching as Miller dropped his cigarette butt on the stoop and crushed it beneath the heel of his shoe. He then waved once more at Nora and went back inside. Nora's smile vanished and she looked at Johnny. "Because I'm committed to a course of action that requires ruthlessness and I have no intention of half-assing it. We need him right now, which means I'll have to keep kissing that fat ass of his for a while. But we'll deal with him at some point after the rest of it's over. In a few weeks, maybe. We wouldn't want his death coinciding with what's about to happen to Lily and the other woman. This way there'll be less chance of the two things being linked."

Johnny was speechless.

There was logic behind the methodology, of course. Again, though, her lack of emotion unnerved him. He could imagine her discussing business strategies with clients in the same tone. A part of her probably saw this whole thing as a natural application of the skillset she'd acquired in her professional career. Where he saw nothing but messy chaos, Nora saw something else—a puzzle that needing solving. And nothing else. There were pieces to be moved around in particular ways and identifiable steps to be followed. The inherent danger inherent in it all didn't bother her because she believed following the steps would negate the danger. And the human part of the equation didn't bother her because...

Well, that was the really unsettling part, wasn't it?

Because she seemed to have no regard for human life whatsoever beyond how it impacted her and the things important to her. It made him wonder if she could dispense with him just as ruthlessly if she eventually decided she no longer wanted him in her life.

Might he one day become an expendable "loose end"?

Oh, for the love of fuck, what have I gotten myself into?

Nora started the Mercedes and pulled it around to a side entrance, which was shielded from street view. She did a three-point turn in the little parking lot and backed the car's rear end up to the entrance, stopping about six feet short of it.

She shut off the engine and glanced at Johnny, smiling as she slid on black sunglasses. "This time you get out."

She popped the trunk latch and stepped out of the car without further explanation.

Johnny got out and cast a wary glance at some of the windows around them. They were in a U-shaped area of the property, which was bracketed one on side by Miller family living quarters and on the other by the business side. The windows were all dark and most were covered by blinds. Not surprising for this time of day. He saw no faces looking out at him, but it was hard to take this as comforting. Maybe no one was watching, but the whole place gave him the creeps. It was too easy to imagine restless spirits stirring somewhere on the premises. The sooner they were done with this piece of gruesome business and on to the *next* piece of gruesome business, the better.

Nora opened the dark-tinted glass entrance door and reached up to slide a bracket into place to keep it open. Johnny saw why a moment later when Barry Miller wheeled out a stretcher and positioned it alongside the trunk.

Nora smiled. "Thank you *so* much for doing this, Barry. We really appreciate it. Don't we, Johnny?"

Johnny forced a smile. "That's right."

Miller nodded. "Anything for Nora."

Though the funeral director didn't address him directly, Johnny inferred from his tone that the man had a decidedly lesser opinion of him.

Johnny decided a world without Barry Miller might not be such a bad thing, after all.

Nora gave Johnny's arm a squeeze. "You boys will handle the physical labor part of this. I'll be on lookout until you're safely inside." She turned toward Johnny and dropped her voice to say, "Behave, please. This will all be over soon."

Johnny watched as Nora crossed the parking lot to stand near the open end of the U, where she would presumably keep an eye out for any unexpected visitors. He couldn't help admiring the smooth grace of her walk. It wasn't the exaggerated slutty strut of a barroom temptress, but it conveyed a devastating sexiness nonetheless.

Barry Miller chuckled. "She's something, ain't she?"

Johnny tried not to glare when he looked at Miller. Up close, the guy looked more like the loathsome slug Nora had originally described. His eyes were a tad too close together and his unusually bushy eyebrows lent him a slight caveman aspect. Or maybe Johnny's instinctive dislike of the man was warping his perceptions. Whatever the case, he didn't much feel like making nice so all he said was, "Yeah."

Miller lifted the trunk lid. "I get it. You're nervous. But you've got nothing to worry about, pal. This ain't the first time I've gotten rid of an inconvenient body."

Johnny was curious despite himself. "Oh, yeah?"

Miller shot a glance at the wrapped-up body before directing a smirk at Johnny. "It ain't a regular part of the business, understand, but it happens now and then. I only do it for people I'd trust with my life. I don't know you, but I've got to believe you're trustworthy because you're tight with Nora. I'd do anything for her." He smiled. "And vice versa, believe me."

Johnny nodded.

This poor shithead really believed Nora loved and valued him. Johnny wondered what the guy would think if he told him she had been plotting his murder just a few minutes earlier. But he thought he already knew the answer to that. Miller wouldn't believe him. Nora didn't care about him at all, but his belief that she did was proof that even creeps weren't immune to the effects of female flattery and attention.

He was surprised to feel a twinge of actual pity for Barry Miller.

Until the guy snapped his fingers in Johnny's face and sneered at him. "Get it together, space cadet. We've got a job to do."

Space cadet?

Johnny couldn't remember the last time he'd heard that one. As insults went, it was kind of old-fashioned. It was something his father might have said in days of yore: "Wake up, space cadet. Time to rake the fuckin' yard."

He was initially too amused to take offense, but amusement faded as the deep lines of Barry Miller's face stretched and hardened, transforming the sneer into a craggy scowl. The expression gave Johnny an unvarnished look at a core of nastiness that hadn't been visible during the man's amiable chat with Nora. This was a guy who had no moral qualms regarding the occasional use of his ostensibly noble business as a front for illicit corpse disposal. It struck him that taking someone like that lightly wasn't at all advisable.

The two of them wrestled the long, sheet-wrapped body out of the trunk and hoisted it onto the stretcher. The corpse was already beginning to stiffen with rigor mortis. It was in a crooked position from being wedged so tightly inside the trunk. Johnny found this disturbing, but Miller was nonchalant about it. He explained that Slick hadn't been dead long enough to become completely rigid. He just needed a little help straightening himself out. Miller had Johnny hang onto the body's ankles while he pressed down on the torso. This resulted in a disquieting creak that mad Johnny's gorge rise.

Miller cackled. "Feel like barfing?"

Johnny choked back the little surge of bile and gave his head a grim shake. "I'm fine. Let's get this over with."

Miller's smile was smug. "First time handling a stiff?"

Johnny plucked a cigarillo out of his breast pocket. "It's not my first time in the presence of a corpse." Here he was thinking not only of poor Jamie Benton, but also of being in the room when various relations passed on, an insight he elected not to share with Miller. The guy didn't deserve any kind of intimate look inside his head. "But, yeah, this is the first time I've been in this kind of situation."

Miller's bushy eyebrows rose at the sight of Johnny's Zippo, which he'd just flipped open. "Put that away. There's no smoking out here. Or inside the building."

"You're shitting me. I saw you smoking on the back stoop."

Miller's tone was stern as he said, "I don't care what you saw. My house, my rules."

The guy was being an ass just for the sake of being an ass. Unfortunately, his services were required and protesting further wasn't an option. Johnny reluctantly put the Zippo away and slipped the cigarillo back inside his pocket. Not being able to drink was bad enough, but also being denied a nicotine fix made a situation that was already borderline unbearable that much worse. He needed something to soothe his nerves and he needed it soon.

Together they wheeled the stretcher through building until they reached the crematory, where Miller took a bit of time getting things set up. After that, Johnny helped him hoist the body onto a table, where Millar began the process of peeling away the duct tape to remove the shroud of bed sheets.

Johnny felt his gorge rise again. "Hold on. The fuck are you doing? Why not just leave him the way he is?"

"I'm checking him for items that need to be removed. Prostheses. Anything metal. Implants or piercings. Whatever. Things that won't burn up easily or that could explode during cremation."

Johnny's eyes widened. "Explode?"

"Sure, like a pacemaker." Miller tugged a double-thickness of sheets away from Slick's head and smirked when he saw the dead man's face. "Way too young for a pacemaker. Help me look for surgical scars."

Johnny grimaced. "Goddammit."

Miller laughed.

There was no getting out of any of this. So Johnny helped Miller with every stage of the process until they reached the point where he was no longer able to assist because he lacked the necessary technical knowledge. Once Slick's remains had been consigned to the furnace, Miller ushered Johnny out of the crematory.

Johnny glanced at the corrupt funeral director as they walked down a long hallway. "How long will it take?"

Miller shrugged. "Skinny guy like that? Couple hours. Get a real fat bastard in there and it could take a lot longer."

Johnny refrained from snide speculation regarding how long it might take Miller to burn up in the crematory furnace

Nora was waiting by the Mercedes as they emerged from the building. She was leaning against the back of the car. Her legs were crossed at her ankles and her right arm was held upright, a smoldering cigarette pinched between two fingers. She was smiling inscrutably beneath her stylish black sunglasses. She looked sleek and sophisticated in her charcoal-colored pencil skirt, dark blue blouse, and black heels. Her whole manner conveyed insouciance, which was odd in light of the danger still facing them.

"All finished, boys?"

Miller chuckled and plucked the cigarette from Nora's fingers. He took a deep drag from it and passed it back to her. "Damn near. There's just that one other thing…"

Nora dropped the cigarette and crushed it beneath a heel. She clasped hands with Miller and smiled brightly at him. "Lead the way, doll."

Johnny glowered as they walked past him and into the funeral home.

He stared at the closed dark-tinted door for a long moment, feeling the rage build inside him. An urge to go back in there and drag Nora out after beating the shit out of Barry Miller nearly overpowered him.

Instead he counted slowly to ten and let out a big breath. He then moved away from the door and sat on the hood of Nora's Mercedes, where he smoked two cigarillos and waited and pondered some of the darkest thoughts to ever cross his mind.

The nicotine didn't help at all.

20

Almost an hour passed before Nora reemerged from the mortuary, this time unaccompanied by Barry Miller. Her clothes were unrumpled and her hair and makeup were perfect again. She had apparently done a touch-up job on both before exiting the building. The black sunglasses were in place and she still exuded grace and poise. A casual observer would never imagine she had just traded a sexual favor for assistance in disposing of a corpse. She looked radiant in the late afternoon sunlight, like a shimmering vision of a silver screen goddess from Hollywood's golden days brought to blazing, full-color life. Johnny couldn't help admiring her almost regal bearing. At the same time, it was another in a series of things a part of him found disturbingly incongruous about her behavior.

She opened the driver's side door and dropped in next to Johnny.

"That took a while."

Nora put a key in the ignition and started the Mercedes. "It took as long as it needed to take."

She put the car in gear and they drove away from the funeral home. It was approaching early evening and the midtown traffic was congested. Nora swung the Mercedes into a passing lane as soon as there was an opening and they headed in the general direction of the square.

Johnny stared out the window on his side at a landscape that was a mix of austere-looking municipal buildings and small businesses. Much of what he saw was unchanged or little-

107

changed from his childhood. On the square things were different, brighter and livelier than they had been decades ago. And there were more people these days. The quirky college town was becoming a bustling little city. He couldn't help wondering whether the accelerated pace of life might in some way be to blame for his current troubles.

Probably not.

And blaming other people or factors for things that were largely his own damn fault was pointless.

Johnny looked at Nora. "Did you fuck him?"

She glanced sharply at him. "Are you accusing me of something?"

"I'm just saying…you were in there over an hour. Must have been some blowjob."

Johnny knew he was being a bit of a petulant child. He had known about the sexual component of their business with Miller from the beginning and was thus in no position to start crying about it now. But he just couldn't help himself.

"Would you like to know exactly what happened?"

Johnny tugged a cigarillo out of his breast pocket. "I would not. In fact, I'm sorry I said anything. Let's just drop it, okay?"

Nora reached over and flicked the cigarillo out of his hand.

"Hey!"

"No smoking in my car."

"Since when?"

"Since now."

Johnny shook his head. "Jesus. Suddenly everybody's got a problem with me smoking."

"It's a nasty habit."

The comment made Johnny splutter. "What the…*you* smoke cigarettes."

"So? My menthols don't stink as much as your little cigars."

"You're just feeling bitchy because I pissed you off."

Nora stomped on the brake pedal and the Mercedes screeched to a halt a few inches shy of a Ford Tempo's rear bumper. There was a red streetlight several car-lengths up ahead. Johnny wasn't sure where they were headed. They would need to be in the right-hand lane to get to the square and this wasn't the most direct route to either of their houses.

"Where--"

Nora whipped off her sunglasses and glared at him. "Barry has performance issues. He got it up after popping a boner pill, but he was never able to come, not even after I fulfilled one of his fantasies by blowing him on an embalming table. The whole thing was a hugely embarrassing farce for both of us. There, Johnny. Now you know exactly what happened. Are you finally ready to stop being such a baby about it?"

Johnny kept his face carefully blank for a moment.

But then he couldn't help it.

He giggled.

"An *embalming* table?"

Nora heaved a weary sigh. "Yes. Fuck. I knew I shouldn't have told you."

Johnny shook his head. "A fucking embalming table. What a freak."

"Oh, please. You're the one who just killed a guy and allowed his girlfriend to prostitute herself in order to get rid of the evidence."

Johnny's grin faded. "Okay. Yeah. Look, I'm sorry. You're probably the only person in the world who would've done that for me and I'm being a whiny asshole about it."

The light up ahead turned green and the Mercedes moved forward until it cycled back to red, at which point they were two car-lengths short of the intersection.

Nora smiled as she looked at him. "I forgive you. And it's okay. It had to be done. Let's drop it and focus on figuring out our next move."

Grim reality came stealing back in with that comment and Johnny felt a flutter of unease tug at his guts. He had been able to put the rest of it out of his mind while he worried about other things—such as what Nora was doing with Barry—but now he was again forced to confront it.

He looked at Nora. "I'm done killing."

"The hell you are." Nora's expression turned harsh and there was something savage in the sharp curl of her mouth. "I didn't just spend the better part of an hour whoring myself out to Barry Miller just to have you chicken out. We're doing this thing and that's the end of it."

Johnny stared straight ahead, his mood more somber than ever. "I don't have a choice is what you're saying."

"You haven't had a choice since the moment you put a bullet in Slick Hogan's head."

Johnny didn't say anything. It was a hard point to counter.

The light turned green again and Nora guided the Mercedes through the intersection. The traffic on the other side was a little lighter and they were able to make it through the next intersection before having to stop again.

Nora's tone was more conciliatory as she said, "You can smoke one of your stinky little cigars."

Johnny had one of his cigarillos lit up and was puffing on it within about five seconds. Nora pushed a button and the window on his side rolled down a few inches. Johnny blew smoke through the narrow opening and looked at her. "Thank you. Now if only I could get a drink."

"You can have one later tonight if things go right."

Johnny hung his head. "Meaning after we murder two human beings."

"I had a thought about that. Maybe we only have to kill one of them."

Johnny looked at her. "Which one?"

"Lily, of course."

Johnny frowned and didn't reply.

"I know you don't like it, but she has to die. And like I told you before, I'll do the actual dirty work this time. But we'll need to separate her from the other one, maybe lure her out somehow and grab her."

Johnny dragged on his cigarillo and blew more smoke out the window. "And how are we supposed to do that?"

"Call her and arrange a meeting."

Johnny's soft laugh was devoid of humor. "Maybe I'm stupid, but that sounds like a really bad idea. As the former spouse, I'll be getting squeezed hard enough by the cops as it is. A record of a phone contact with her the day she disappears would look mighty fucking suspicious."

Nora smiled. "So it's a good thing I took Slick's phone off him before we got rid of him."

Johnny arched an eyebrow. "You did? Where is it?"

"In your desk, along with his gun. I figured both items might come in handy later."

Nora rolled through yet another intersection and suddenly they were speeding along on a longer, more wide-open stretch of road. Johnny flicked the half-smoked cigarillo out the window and in a moment there was a soft hum as the window closed.

"Okay, let's say I call her from Slick's phone. There's no record of me calling her. That's good. But Lily will lose her shit. She'll figure out something's happened to her boyfriend, or whatever he was to her, and she'll get scared, maybe decide to let this crazy friend of hers in on what's happening."

Nora shook her head. "I don't think so. From what you tell me, this Bree person has a nasty temper."

Johnny grunted. "That's the understatement of the goddamn century."

Nora nodded. "Lily may have questionable judgment, but she's not stupid. She won't risk letting a psycho like Bree know she and Slick worked out this little deal behind her back. And there's something else you're not considering."

"Oh, yeah? What's that?"

Nora smiled. "This is the beauty part. We'll just text her."

Johnny's features went slack for a moment.

Then he shook his head. "Fucking hell. Why didn't I think of that?"

Nora chuckled. "Because I'm the brains of this operation. Obviously."

They drove in near silence the rest of the way back to Johnny's house. It was a heavy, contemplative silence. Nora smiled in a speculative way as they turned down the street leading to his house. Despite everything, he smiled in return. The sense that they would be spending some quality time in his bedroom soon was strong. It would be just the thing to break up some of the nervous tension they were both feeling.

But the growing erotic charge abruptly fizzled as they neared his house.

Nora frowned and leaned forward in her seat. "Is that..."

She didn't need to finish the question.

Johnny shook his head in amazement.

Speak of the devil...

Lily's Honda Civic was parked in his driveway.

And she was sitting on his porch.

Waiting for him.

21

Lily stood up as Nora pulled into the driveway and parked behind the Austin-Healey. She was wearing denim cut-offs, a white tank top, and sandals. Oversized sunglasses of the type favored by modern day pop divas hid her eyes. Her long dark hair fell in lustrous waves to the tops of her breasts. From a distance, her long-legged, willowy look still held a lot of its old power.

Nora glanced at Johnny. "Did I ever tell you I made out with her once?"

Johnny did a double-take. "What?"

Nora smiled. "It was when we were all still working at First Mortgage together. You had a Halloween party here one year..."

Johnny winced. "I remember that party. Up to a certain point."

"You got hammered and passed out. Shocking, right?"

Johnny scowled. "I get it. I'm a drunk. You don't have to keep throwing it in my face."

"This happened after you were down for the count," Nora said, ignoring his comment. "Hours later, actually, like deep into the morning. Lily was pretty trashed herself at that point. Anyway, there were still a few people keeping it going. Drinking and dancing. And out of nowhere, Lily grabs me and sticks her tongue down my throat.."

An image that was not repulsive formed in Johnny's head.

"Huh."

Nora smacked his arm. "Fucking perv. Anyway…it wasn't the worst thing ever, I'll say that. She tasted nice."

Johnny shifted in his seat. "Huh."

"She tried to drag me off to a bedroom, but I didn't let her. The kissing was okay, but I wasn't into going anywhere else with it. We were always awkward around each other after that."

That was something else Johnny remembered. They'd all been tight those first few years together at First Mortgage, but things turned frosty after the Halloween party. He hadn't understood it at the time and had sensed there was something he was being kept in the dark about. Things stayed that way until Nora left and took the loan officer position at the bank.

But now everything was clicking into place. Lily had been a popular and highly-valued member of the team during her time at First Mortgage, thanks largely to her beauty and engaging personality. So when she decided to freeze Nora out, many of their co-workers followed suit. Now Johnny knew why, though he still didn't fully understand it. Nora had rejected a drunken sexual advance at a party. So what? Those things happened. And when they did, most people wrote it off as the usual kind of boozy shenanigans that sometimes went down at such gatherings and moved on. There was no good reason to take it as some kind of unforgiveable insult.

That Lily was capable of being extraordinarily petty wasn't exactly a revelation. And yet there was a small—albeit ever-dwindling—part of him that still wanted to think well of her. It was there despite knowing she had conspired with Slick against him. He sometimes told himself it was a new thing, this pettiness, but of course that was bullshit.

It had always been a part of her.

He had just blinded himself to it.

Nora opened the door on her side and swung a leg out. "Let's see what she has to say for herself."

She was out of the car before Johnny could reply. It was disconcerting. He'd assumed they would first take a minute to discuss how to deal with Lily. Either Nora already had some sort of rudimentary plan in mind—one she hadn't elected to share with Johnny—or she was just throwing caution to the wind. The latter possibility didn't sound like the Nora he knew. Then again, she had been surprising him a lot lately. It was exasperating and unsettling, but what could he do about it?

Nothing, except follow her lead and hope for the best.

Johnny got out of the Mercedes and followed Nora down the sidewalk.

Lily stood at the edge of the porch with her hands on her hips. She looked angry. A large purse with long leather straps was threatening to slide off her shoulder. Johnny felt a jolt of apprehension at the thought that she might be concealing a gun inside it. He'd already let someone with a gun get the drop on him once today and he was in no hurry to relive the experience.

But it wasn't like he could turn tail and run. Nora would definitely break things off with him if he left her to face Lily alone. And he didn't want that to happen, despite knowing how cold and ruthless she was capable of being. So he kept pace with her and fell into position next to her when they reached the porch.

Lily leveled an icy glare at Johnny. "You changed locks on me."

Johnny's brow creased. "Uh, yeah...I did."

"I'll need a new key."

Johnny scratched the back of his head. "Um...well, the thing is--"

"You're not getting a new key," Nora interjected, her pleasant tone belying her defiant words. "You don't live here anymore and you can't drop in whenever you please."

Lily thrust her chin at Nora. "You need to leave, bitch. I have to talk to Johnny in private."

Nora smiled. "Afraid I can't let that happen, Lily. You want to talk to Johnny, you'll have to talk to me, too."

Lily stepped off the porch and approached Nora until they were standing no more than a foot apart. She swept off her sunglasses and leaned even closer. "Leave," she said, her tone low and menacing, "or I'll kick the shit out of you."

Nora glanced at Johnny. "Come on, baby. Let's go have that drink you've been wanting."

Before Johnny could say anything, she brushed past Lily and climbed the steps to the porch. Johnny moved to follow her—the promise of a drink being the only prompt he needed—but Lily moved to intercept him.

She gripped him by a bicep and fixed him with a glare that was equal parts disbelief and incipient rage. "Tell me you're not fucking that whore. You're not, are you, Johnny?"

Johnny gently pried his arm free from Lily's grip and joined Nora on the porch.

He heard Lily grunt. "Did you seriously just walk away from me, motherfucker?"

Johnny dug his keys out of his hip pocket and was surprised to see his hand shaking a little. He realized at once the shakiness was a combination of Lily's physical proximity and the anger she was directing at him. He knew it was stupid of him, but it hurt hearing her lashing out at him like that. There was no recognizable trace left of the woman he had loved. He should hate her the way Nora wanted him to hate her.

Yet he didn't.

He couldn't.

It just wasn't in him. And he had no clue how he could possibly be expected to go along with any plan to kill her when she was still able to exert this kind of emotional pull on him.

Johnny willed his hand to stop shaking and managed to avoid dropping the keys. He located the new house key and unlocked the door. Lily kept yelling at them as she followed them into the house. The verbal barrage didn't let up as they continued through the foyer to the living room.

Johnny was on the verge of finally responding when Nora intervened.

"We'll discuss whatever you want shortly." She took off her sunglasses and smiled, looking almost impossibly calm. "But first Johnny will fetch us drinks. A beer for himself and a vodka martini for me. What would you like, Lily?"

Lily sneered. "I'll have a fucking beer."

Nora turned her serene smile on Johnny. "You heard the lady. Get her a fucking beer."

Johnny hurried off to the kitchen, where he took a couple beers from the fridge and set them on the counter after prying off their tops with an opener shaped like a stripper's curvy, stocking-covered leg. Before preparing Nora's vodka drink, he grabbed a whiskey bottle and took a long swig from it. The hell with this being forced to lay off the hard stuff nonsense. Nothing less than strong whiskey could soothe his nerves at this point. He took one more big gulp from the bottle and got to work on Nora's drink.

He wished he knew what Nora had in mind. She might well be planning to kill Lily here and now, while they had her in their grasp. While Johnny didn't want it to happen at all, he understood the temptation to do it now and have it done. They could then get back in touch with Barry Miller and negotiate the disposal of one more body, after which this would all be over and they could go back to their normal lives.

Except for one little thing.

They had talked about being careful, about avoiding anything that put them with Lily around the time of her disappearance. It was the whole reason they'd agreed not to use his phone to contact her. But now here she was in his house. Darkness was still a couple hours away and her car was sitting in his driveway for anyone to see. And who knew how long she had been waiting on his porch? His neighbors weren't particularly nosy, but even people who mostly mind their own business will notice things after a while.

Johnny stared at his hands.

They were shaking again. He wouldn't be any good in the conversation that was about to happen if he couldn't get a grip. He opened his mouth and let out a breath. He tilted his head back and stared at the ceiling, focusing on nothing but breathing in and out for a few moments

When he thought he had his nerves firmly under control again, he carried the drinks out to the living room. Nora had kicked off her shoes and was sitting on the sofa with her legs tucked beneath her. She accepted the martini glass with a grateful smile and sipped almost daintily from it.

Apparently too agitated to sit, Lily was pacing back and forth across the living room, the soles of her sandals flapping on the hardwood floor. When Johnny proffered one of the beers, she ripped it from his hand and drank deeply from it. "Where the fuck is Slick?"

Johnny frowned. "What?"

Lily's laughter had a savage edge to it. "Don't even play with me, asshole. Slick's Nova is still parked on the square. He hasn't answered his phone all afternoon. The last I knew he was here with you. So where is he?"

Johnny shook his head. "I don't--"

Lily got right up to his face. "Don't lie to me." She spoke more softly now, but the quieter tone did nothing to blunt the hard edge of her words. "I've put up with your shit so far, but that won't last much longer. Tell me what happened before I really get angry."

Johnny couldn't help it.

Her warm breath against his face was almost making him swoon. He felt his fragile resolve slipping away as he glanced at Nora. Her expression was neutral, the studious look of an outside observer, which was incredibly unnerving.

He needed her to leap in here and rescue him.

Why wasn't she doing that?

Lily put a hand against his cheek and forced him to focus on her. "Don't look at her, look at me."

Johnny swallowed hard. "Lily--"

"Tell me the truth, Johnny. *Now.*"

Johnny met her gaze and thought about all the countless times he'd peered lovingly into her eyes during their married life. Her hand was still touching his cheek. It was a light, almost gentle touch. He experienced a moment of powerful déjà vu and a kaleidoscope of memories from better times flashed through his head. He felt like he would either faint or blurt out everything.

Then the moment passed.

"You want the truth? Fine. Here it is. And remember, I tried to spare you this."

Lily's face twisted in a scowl. "The fuck are you babbling about?"

Johnny moved away from her and took up a position at the side of the sofa closest to Nora. He drank from his beer and arranged his features in an expression of fake pity. "I gave Slick the money from the safe, but I told him I could do even better than that if he let me live. At first he wasn't buying it, but I convinced him I could make it worth his while."

Lily snorted. "Bullshit."

Johnny shook his head. "It's not bullshit. I made him believe I could put my hands on a hundred-thousand cash."

Lily laughed. "And how did you do that?"

Johnny smiled. "By showing him my savings account online. I doubt Slick ever imagined he'd see that much money at one time in his life. He wanted it bad. You could see it in his eyes. And all he had to do to get it was let me live and agree to a couple conditions. And he agreed to them pretty fast."

Lily's eyes narrowed as she tried to read him. Something subtle changed in her expression during that moment. Johnny recognized it as the beginning of belief. "What motherfucking conditions?"

"I told him he had to get out of town."

A jolt of panic registered on Lily's face. Her eyes were wide open again and a nervous tic was visible at the hollow of her throat. "That's a fucking lie. Slick wouldn't skip town without telling me."

Johnny nodded in faux-sympathy. "Ordinarily, maybe. But it was another of my conditions. I told him if I gave him the money, he had to leave right away and without contacting you."

Lily stared at him in almost stupefied silence for a while. Her eyes flickered with what might have been desperation. There were gaping holes in his story, but he was counting on Lily's emotions blinding her against them. She was in love with Slick. It was a thing Johnny couldn't fathom, but the truth of it was there in her glistening eyes. He felt a touch of genuine sympathy for her as he watched her struggle with what she was hearing.

Her bottom lip trembled. "Why would you do that, Johnny? You never used to be so cruel."

Lily accusing him of emotional cruelty was a comment rich in irony, but Johnny elected to let it pass without argument. The temptation to revisit old wounds was strong. However, he knew doing so would undercut his ability to sell Lily on this bit of off-the-cuff fiction.

"I did it for your own good. I've been worried about you for a long time. I saw an opportunity to remove a bad influence from your life and acted on it." Johnny spoke with a quiet authority unusual for him. It took him a moment to recognize the tone as derived from memories of his father, a man with a natural talent for making people see things his way. "Now that he's gone, I'm hoping you'll be able to start getting your life in order."

Lily wiped away a tear. "You bastard."

Johnny had an urge to go to her and comfort her. He didn't feel good about making her cry, regardless of what she'd done. But the approving look Nora gave him helped firm up his burgeoning pragmatism. This *had* to be done. Causing her some pain now would be worthwhile if it meant getting her to buy his story. And if he could make *that* happen—make her truly believe in it with all her heart—maybe he could persuade Nora to rethink killing her.

More tears came.

Lily swiped them away with a fierceness that hinted at a dormant strength. She even managed a smile when they finally stopped falling. "What about the car? Why leave it?"

Johnny shrugged. "That was his doing. He took a cab out to the airport."

Lily frowned. "What? The fucking airport? Why?"

"He said something about wanting to get somewhere far away, some place where he could really start over. Somewhere out on the west coast, maybe. Far enough, anyway, that taking his shitty old Nova would be a waste of time. With the money he has now, he can buy a better ride once he gets where he's going."

Johnny struggled not to smile. For something made up on the spot in the midst of a high-stress situation, his bullshit story was coming together in a pretty believable way. And he knew Lily had bought it completely when she started crying again. But he felt another twinge of painful empathy as he watched her shoulders move while she hung her head and quietly sobbed.

Then she looked up and again wiped tears away. "That son of a bitch. I can't believe he did this to me. *Goddammit.*"

This time Johnny did take a tentative step in her direction, but Nora stopped him with a firm hand on his arm.

Lily stomped a foot on the hardwood floor. "*That fucking bastard!*"

She dipped a hand in her purse and Johnny tensed for a moment, remembering his earlier fear that she might be concealing a gun inside it. He let out a relieved breath when she pulled out a cell phone instead. But his relief was short-lived when she tapped some buttons and put the phone to her ear.

She paced furiously about the room again and shot an angry glare at Johnny. "That motherfucker better start answering my calls soon and let me know what's up himself or I *will* track him down wherever's he's gone and make him fucking sorry."

Johnny shot a worried look at Nora.

But Nora's face was a mask of icy calm as she rose from the sofa.

Lily abruptly stopped pacing. She tilted her head as she took the cell phone away from her ear. "Hold on. What is that...is that..."

She frowned and began to walk slowly toward an archway at the far end of the living room. Through the archway was a hallway that would eventually lead to Johnny's office.

Where Slick's phone was stored in a drawer along with his gun.

Lily stood just outside the archway and cast a wide-eyed glance over her shoulder at Johnny and Nora. The sound they were all hearing was muted but recognizable. It was a snippet of a Carl Perkins rockabilly song from the 50's—Slick's dial tone.

Lily's eyes were shining again. "No. No. Slick!"

She dashed through the archway.

Johnny and Nora gave chase.

22

By the time Lily got to the office the ringtone had ceased playing, but she had already honed in one the source of the sound. She went right to Johnny's desk, yanked open the top drawer, and started rooting around inside it. She tossed some manila file folders over her shoulder. Papers flew from the folders and went fluttering to the floor. Evidently Nora had hidden the gun and phone beneath some things, which was smart thinking on her part. It gave Johnny just enough time to get to Lily before she could get her hands on them. The phone he no longer cared about because that part of the game was up. Lily now knew something bad had happened to Slick. His only goal at this point was to keep her from getting the gun.

He grabbed her by an arm and yanked her away from the desk. She dropped her phone and turned toward him to rake her long nails across his face, shredding skin. Only one cut went deep enough to draw blood and the pain wasn't enough to make him relinquish his grip on her. But her hand went right back to his face and this time she was going for his eyes.

Johnny let go of her and reeled backward, crashing into the tall bookcase that housed his safe and most-prized hardbound volumes. He hit it with enough force that he felt the safe's combination dial gouge into the flesh between his shoulder blades. The back of the bookcase struck the wall and when Johnny pitched forward a number of books tumbled off the shelves and thumped on the floor.

Lily started rifling through the drawer again.

Nora picked up a fallen book and winged it across the desk at Lily. The thick hardcover volume struck Lily in the forehead hard enough to make her topple over on her ass, landing with a resounding crash on the floor behind the desk.

Johnny came at her again, but he stopped short when he saw she had Slick's gun clutched in her right hand. Her disorientation was the only reason Johnny didn't right then. Though she hadn't managed yet to bring the barrel of the gun to bear on him, she unhesitatingly squeezed off a shot that punched a hole in the ceiling. Johnny dove out of the way as she tried to correct her aim and fired again.

Nora was in motion as Johnny hit the floor, displaying astonishing courage as she moved through the potential field of fire and slid a hand behind the bookcase Johnny had nearly knocked over moments ago. She gave it a hard shove and it toppled over. Lily tried to scramble out of the way, but there wasn't time. The heavy steel safe slid off the middle shelf and thudded on the floor next to her an instant before the bookcase landed atop her. She cried out in pain and fired the gun from beneath the bookcase. Holes appeared in its back panel as slugs ripped through it and subsequently embedded themselves in the ceiling.

Johnny's heart was thudding in overdrive when the gun finally clicked empty.

He let out a huge breath of relief and said, "Holy fucking Christ."

Nora approached him and extended a hand. "Get up. We're not done yet."

Johnny's eyes flicked to the fallen bookcase. From his vantage point, he could see the back end of it protruding from where it had fallen behind the desk. He rolled his head to the right as far as he could and looked under his desk. Now he saw Lily pinned beneath the bookcase. She was still conscious and was struggling to get free. He would have known this even without the visual evidence because she was shrieking nonstop. The sound was similar to the piercing cries of bratty children sometimes heard in grocery stores or other public places. It was a sound that made you close your eyes and hope like hell would end soon.

In this case, though, there was no scolding parent to make it stop.

Johnny let Nora help him to his feet. They circled the desk from opposite sides and warily approached the toppled-over bookcase. When he saw Lily this time, Johnny's first thought was that what he saw reminded him of the scene in the film version of *The Wizard of Oz* in which the Wicked Witch of the East is crushed beneath Dorothy's house when it falls on her.

Lily's legs were sticking out from beneath the bookcase and most of her torso was hidden beneath it. The bookcases in Johnny's office weren't the cheap, prefabricated kind available at big box stores. They were tall and handmade with wide, heavy shelves. He wouldn't have much enjoyed having one of them fall over on him and Lily was much more slightly built than he was. Factor in all the heavy hardcover volumes the shelves had contained and it added up to a deeply unpleasant experience.

Johnny looked at Nora. "What now?"

Nora took a quick glance around the office. Her eyebrows went up when she spied something that interested her. It was in a glass display case mounted on the wall opposite the desk. She approached the case and ran a hand along its underside until she found a latch. The latch clicked open with a flick of her thumb. She opened the case and removed the item displayed inside it.

Johnny frowned. "What are you doing with that?"

There was no discernible emotion in Nora's expression, but an unyielding grim determination was evident in her tone when she spoke. "Haul that thing off her and I'll bash her head in with this."

Johnny made no move to do as instructed. "That's a one-of-a-kind Louisville Slugger model autographed by Pete Rose. It's worth a lot."

Nora sniffed. "Well, now you'll finally get some real return on your investment. For fuck's sake, Johnny, I'm tired of listening to that screeching bitch. Move that goddamn bookcase and let's finish this."

She gaped at him in disbelief when he instead approached her and pried the bat from her hands. He returned it to the display case and latched the case shut.

Nora's expression turned disdainful. "Unbelievable. It's just a piece of fucking wood. I can't believe--"

The argument came to an abrupt end as Lily went flashing by them, having managed to wriggle free while they were distracted. Nora cursed and was the first to pick up the pursuit. Johnny just stood there a moment and stared at the open door to the office in stunned disbelief. He grimaced in anticipation of the extreme amount of shit Nora would give him for this later. The sound of feminine shrieks followed by the crash of something toppling over snapped him out of it and sent him running out of the office.

Lily had managed to reach the foyer before Nora caught up to her. The shattered remnants of a vase were scattered across the marble floor tiles. The vase had belonged to Lily and was one of the very many things she'd left behind in her haste to extricate herself from Johnny's life. Seeing it in ruins seemed somehow symbolic of their shattered union. Johnny guessed it had gotten knocked off the display stand when Nora intercepted Lily on her way to the door.

Now the two women were locked in desperate hand-to-hand combat. They were screeching as they slapped and clawed at each other and banged about the room. At one point Nora got the upper hand and managed to slam Lily into a glass curio cabinet. The glass insets shattered and several shards nicked Lily's flesh, drawing trickles of blood. Sensing weakness, Nora lunged in for the kill, but Lily got her hands up in time to protect herself. A thumb went into one of Nora's eyes and gouged hard. Nora screamed in sudden pain as she let go of Lily and reeled away from her.

Lily made another break for the door.

Johnny charged after her, porcelain shards crunching beneath his boots as he ran. Lily got her hands around the doorknob and managed to wrench the door open less than a second before he reached her. She screamed as he seized her about the waist and kicked the door shut. He lifted her off her feet and moved backward, hoping fervently he wouldn't slip on any of the vase shards.

He didn't want this—had never wanted it—but things had gone too far now. A man was dead and Lily knew it. The circumstantial evidence she'd discovered left little doubt on that count. Simply letting her go was no longer an option. Sure, she wouldn't be in any hurry to go to the cops thanks to Johnny's knowledge of Jamie Benton's murder, but Lily wouldn't just let this go. She would want revenge and Johnny was sure she would put aside any reservations she might have had about involving that psycho friend of hers in order to get it.

Lily flailed and kicked her legs in the air as Johnny carried her into the living room. Her wild gyrations made him stagger side to side and at one point he only managed to remain upright when they fell toward a wall. Lily's feet slapped against the wall and she tried to use her leverage to propel them backward hard enough to dislodge Johnny's grip on her. But Johnny was already moving backward before she could make that happen. Her feet slid across a framed photo of his parents taken on some long ago beach vacation. The picture came off its hook and fell to the floor with a sound of breaking glass.

Johnny at last managed to get her over to the sofa. He threw her down and pinned her to the sofa with a knee pressed hard against the small of her back. He held onto her shoulders to help keep her from wriggling around too much. She screamed and tried to claw at him, but her position on the sofa made reaching him difficult.

Nora was standing over them at the side of the sofa now. "She's making too much noise."

Johnny was panting hard as he looked up at her. "You think I don't know that? I don't know how to make her stop."

Nora stooped to retrieve a throw pillow that had been knocked to the floor. She seized a handful of Lily's hair, lifted her head up, and slid the pillow under her. She then pressed Lily's face into the pillow, bearing down hard with both hands gripping the back of her head. Lily flailed harder than ever and screeched some more. The pillow muffled the sound effectively, but a shudder of revulsion rippled through Johnny as he realized he and Nora were now working together to kill Lily. This was no longer about subduing or reasoning with her. It was about *ending* her. After all that had gone down today, it was the only logical endgame.

And yet he just couldn't go through with it, not when it got down to the real moment of truth. The struggling woman beneath him was someone he'd made love to countless hundreds of times. He'd cherished her and held her in his arms so many blissful evenings. All that was gone, part of an earlier life he could never get back, but it still had to count for something.

Right?

He ripped the pillow from under Lily's head and she immediately drew in a great, ragged, gasping breath. Then she started sobbing and shaking beneath him. Johnny looked at her trapped body and was overcome with self-loathing. He felt like a filthy rapist holding down a victim he was about to violate.

Then he was in pain as Nora's hand cracked across his face.

"What the fuck are you doing, you goddamn idiot?"

Johnny winced as he touched his burning cheek. "I can't do it. I can't kill her."

A look of deep disgust twisted Nora's face. "Don't be an ass. There's no room for emotion here. It *has* to be done. And you know it."

Johnny shook his head. "There has to be another way."

"There isn't. This isn't just about you anymore, Johnny. My life isn't getting ruined over this and that's exactly what'll happen if we let her live." Nora started moving away from him. "You keep her right where she is until I get back."

"What are you doing?"

"Getting something from the kitchen to finish this." Both her tone and expression were severe. "Do *not* let her up, Johnny."

And then she was gone.

Lily turned her head to the side and her eyes rolled up to look at him. Her face was blotchy and her eyes were bright with tears. There were so many tears they were dampening the cushion beneath her. Her breath hitched and her face crumpled as she tried to talk to him. "Please. Johnny. Please. Please...please let me go."

Terror had replaced rage in her expression and he couldn't cope with knowing he was the cause of it. It made him feel less than human. This was a feeling that had been recurring much of the day, ever since he'd pumped two bullets into Slick's body and watched him bleed out. But now the feeling was accompanied by a mounting sense that things would never be right again. This was the end of everything. The flesh was still living, but the old Johnny Doyle was gone forever.

Lily sniffled. "Please. Please. Johnny...I won't tell anyone. I promise. I know you're a good man. I know you never stopped loving me. I'm so sorry for everything. Just please...*please* let me live."

Johnny relaxed his grip on her a little.

Yes. Let her live. It's the right thing to do.

And he might actually have let her up if Nora hadn't returned from the kitchen at that very moment.

Clutched in her right hand was a butcher's knife.

23

The butcher's knife's large, heavy blade was shiny and lethal-looking.

Johnny gasped at the sight of it. "Whoa. Hold on. What do you mean to do with that?"

Nora gave him a look of deep disdain. It was a look that said she'd never heard anything so stupid. "Kill her with it. What do you think?"

Lily whimpered, sounding more pitiful than ever.

Johnny shook his head. "You can't do that."

"And why not?"

Johnny knew convincing Nora to spare Lily's life would be almost impossible. She was convinced her own life—as well as her standing in the community—would be in jeopardy if she allowed that to happen. But maybe he could put her off at least a few more minutes and hope some viable alternative option occurred to him before it was too late. That option remained elusive, but a legitimate delaying tactic did occur to him.

He looked Nora steadily in the eye and said, "Think of all the blood. The sofa will be ruined. It'll be a huge fucking mess and cleaning it up will be impossible."

Nora nodded. "I thought of that. That's why we'll do it in the bathroom. You'll hold her down in the tub while I cut her throat. After she's dead, we'll just wash the blood down the drain." A chilling smile touched the corners of her mouth. "No muss, no fuss."

The matter-of-fact way she said it disturbed Johnny almost as much as that cold little smile. He didn't know why it should at this point. Everything she was saying was in line with her already established behavior pattern. He guessed some part of him kept hoping she would eventually display some slight evidence of moral qualms. It was past time to give up hope on that count, just as he had with everything else.

Nora narrowed her eyes as she studied him closely. "Something wrong, Johnny?"

He held her gaze for a long, uncomfortable moment. A powerful impulse to say what he really thought hammered at him with a force that wouldn't be denied. She wouldn't like it, but he knew he wouldn't be able to forgive himself later if he didn't make himself say the words.

"I don't think we should kill her."

Nora's hard expression gave way to a rage-fueled glower. "Are you fucking shitting me?" She jerked her head in a spastic way, her eyes bulging from their sockets as she waved the big knife around and spat out the words. "You know we have to fucking do this! You agreed it was the right goddamn thing to do!"

Johnny's heart was pounding the way it always did in moments of high drama and agitation. He frequently had trouble dealing with emotionally distressed women even when the stakes weren't life and death. But he also felt a gathering sense of calm that was getting stronger by the second. The reason why was obvious. He'd found his courage and made himself say what needed saying. He had done the right thing. Now he had to hold on to that courage and see this through to the end.

"I agreed to nothing. Not really. You steamrolled me into going along with it. You had your reasons, I know, reasons that make sense in a way. If you have no soul or don't value human life at all, that is."

Nora stared at him in open-mouthed shock for a moment. Then she laughed. "Jesus Christ. I was gone for, what, two minutes? That's all the time this bitch needed to get to you?

Where's your fucking common sense, Johnny?" She laughed again and shook her head. "I'll tell you what. Before anything else happens, you take a few moments and think hard about the real consequences of letting her go. Just put emotion entirely aside and really *think* about it for a few minutes. We've come this far, I think you owe me that at least. Can you do that for me, Johnny?"

Johnny stared at her as a couple of hellishly long, tense minutes elapsed. This was only for show. His mind was made up. "Okay. I've thought about it. Now you listen to me for a minute." His gaze flicked briefly to Lily, who had shifted position on the couch now that he had significantly relaxed his hold on her. She was on her back and his knee was pressed lightly against her stomach. There was a glint of hope in her eyes as she stared up at him. "Lily, I killed Slick. You already guessed that, I'm sure. And I'm real fucking sorry about that. Killing a man isn't something I ever wanted to do. But it was a necessary act of self-defense. I can be at peace with it someday."

This elicited a loud snort from Nora. "Oh, please. I can guess where you're going with this and it is pure bullshit. Let me remind you that Lily is not innocent in this. She knew Slick meant to kill you. Oh, and apparently you've forgotten, but she was fucking *shooting* at us just a few minutes ago! Jesus, Johnny, the booze is turning your brain to mush."

Johnny just let her words roll over him. There was a lot of truth in them. But it was a truth he no longer cared much about. It meant nothing next to that awful sense of self-loathing he'd felt as he'd held Lily down and felt the primal force of her terror seeping into him, filling him like poison.

He met Lily's gaze as he picked up where he'd left off. What he was saying was almost entirely for her benefit now, anyway. "I killed Slick because the only other choice was to take a bullet in the head. In your heart, Lily, I think even you can't blame me for that. There's nothing to be done about it. He can't be brought back. Just as Jamie Benton can never be brought back."

Lily's eyes widened a little. "You know her name?"

Johnny nodded. "We both know some things about each other we wouldn't want other people knowing about. The way I see it, we ought to just leave it at that. Call it even and go on with our lives. I'll even give you the money Slick came here to take, if that helps."

"This is nonsense you're talking, Johnny." Nora's voice was thick with disgust. "It's suicidal. You might as well put a gun to your head and pull the trigger."

Johnny shook his head and kept looking at Lily. "There's no reason it has to be like that. What do you say, Lily? Can we work this out?"

A tentative smile dimpled the edges of Lily's mouth. There was a hint of something cagey in it, which was mildly disturbing, but she seemed a whole lot more calm now. The truth was, he had no idea whether he could trust her to hold up her end of his proposed bargain, but he was willing to take a leap of faith. There was a chance it would mean serious trouble down the road, but that was a chance he was ready to take.

"I'm sorry about Slick, Johnny. I really am." Lily's tone had a mildly plaintive tinge to it, the kind you'd aim for if you were trying to fake sincerity. "The whole thing was his idea. You don't know what he's like." She paused to sniffle. "What he *was* like, I mean. Once he got an idea in his head, changing his mind was impossible. And he got awful mad at me if I tried to go against him. He beat me and threatened me. He...he..."

Nora groaned. "The hell with this bullshit."

She let out a screech and dove toward the couch, swinging the knife in a vicious downward arc at Lily. Johnny reacted by putting himself between the two women. This was nothing but pure, unthinking instinct. The knife cut through his Hawaiian shirt and scraped across his shoulder, tracing a line of fire through his flesh several inches long. He grimaced and cried out as the blood began to flow. Nora screamed in recognition of what she'd done and dropped the knife, staggering backward.

Then she made a sound of deep anguish and said "Oh, my God" over and over.

Lily made a nearly inaudible sound that *might* have been very soft laughter.

Johnny thumped down on the edge of the sofa and clamped a hand against his wound. Blood spilled between his shaking fingers and stained his shirt before dripping to the floor. Lily swung her legs around and sat up next to him. She pulled his hand aside and peered at the wound. She winced and said, "Get that shirt off. I'll get some towels and first aid stuff from the bathroom."

She slid off the couch and scooped up the bloody knife as she got to her feet. Nora let out a startled gasp and took another couple of staggering backward steps. Lily smiled but made no threatening move in her direction. "I'll take care of him, Nora. But I think you should leave. You've done enough damage for one night."

Nora looked at Johnny beseechingly. "I'm sorry I hurt you, but please don't listen to this bitch. You know you can't trust her. And you sure as hell can't be alone with her."

Johnny looked at her with hooded eyes, gritting his teeth as he trembled against the pain. "You're right. I can't trust her. But she won't kill me. Not tonight."

Nora's eyes registered disbelief. "*How* can you know that?"

In truth, Johnny didn't know it. His gut told him he was safe for tonight, but his gut was often wrong, especially lately. Still, the sense that he had nothing to fear from Lily for the time being was strong. His breath hissed through his clenched teeth as he shook his head. "It doesn't matter. But I do think you should go."

Nora looked hurt, her features crumpling. ":Johnny--"

He held up a shaky hand in a placating gesture. "It isn't personal. I still like you. But we've both been through a lot today. Go home and get some rest. I'll see you tomorrow. Okay?"

Nora stared at him and said nothing for several moments. As she did, the sense that she was on the verge of tears went away and her face became a carefully guarded blank mask. She then moved about the room gathering up her things. She stepped into her shoes and slipped the strap of her purse over a shoulder.

The blank look slipped for a moment when she faced Lily, a sliver of palpable hatred appearing. "Anything happens to him, you die."

She walked out of the house without another word, slamming the door behind her.

Lily stared in the direction of the foyer for a moment, an inscrutable smile playing at the edges of her mouth.

Then she looked at Johnny and smiled more broadly. "Stupid cunt."

24

Lily slipped the tip of the blade under Johnny's chin and gave it a gentle upward nudge to make him look her in the eye. Her demeanor was calm and she looked amused in a strangely detached way. There was, however, a faint undercurrent of menace in the way she was looking at him. Her eyes were clearer than he'd seen them in a while and the stench of alcohol that normally hung about her like a toxic cloud was missing.

"I could kill you, Johnny." She said this without overt malice, in the monotone of a bored student regurgitating a nugget of information committed to rote memory. "I really could. I could cut your throat right now." She gave him another little nudge with the knife, making him wince. "And you wouldn't be able to do anything about it."

She didn't say anything else, just tilted her head and waited to see how he'd react.

Johnny resisted the urge to cringe away from the inch of cold steel pressing firmly against his vulnerable flesh. "I know you could."

He said nothing else. There was nothing else *to* say. Either she would kill him or she wouldn't. He felt fear at the prospect, of course, but it was remote. His curiosity about which way she would go was felt more acutely than his fear.

Lily lowered the knife and smiled softly. "Get that shirt off. I'll be right back."

She set the knife on the coffee table and walked out of the room.

Johnny watched her go and then turned his attention to the knife. Much of the shiny blade was obscured by dark blood. There was enough of it that knowing it came from his wounded flesh made him queasy. He recalled the sensation of the blade slicing so easily into him and got even queasier. The part of him that still put some value on self-preservation belatedly scolded him for his impulsive act of intervention, pointing out that Nora could easily have killed him if the blade had gone in just a few inches in another direction. He still had difficulty believing he'd actually done it. It had been either a very brave thing to do or a very foolhardy one. Probably it had been a bit of both. He hadn't been guilty of actual bravery often in his life. And like those rare other times, there had been no thought involved at all.

"Brave" certainly wasn't the word Nora would use to describe what he had done. She thought he was being stupid and impetuous. The hell of it was, she wasn't wrong. Despite everything he'd said, there was no sense in the course he'd chosen from a standpoint of pure pragmatism. It was a huge risk. The way Lily had taunted him with the knife starkly underlined that point. He would be vulnerable every second spent alone in this house with her. He knew what Nora would tell him if she could hear these thoughts. She would say anything that happened to him would be his fault. That he was getting what he deserved for being so goddamned weak-willed and, yes, stupid.

He thought of how he'd sent her from his house and felt a pang of deep regret. This brought a soft grunt of humorless laughter. Christ, he couldn't get his head running smoothly in any one direction. He was a man conflicted, eaten alive by doubt and second thoughts. Nora's lack of a discernible conscience was a real issue. The notion of any kind of real relationship with a person untroubled by murder was absurd.

Or was it?

Sociopaths thrived at all levels of society and were capable of maintaining healthy, successful relationships. He had read this somewhere. Maybe it was true and maybe it wasn't, but one thing was undeniable—he liked Nora and felt a sense of genuine connection with her.

He frowned.

Shit. How do I fix this?

"I told you to take off that shirt."

Johnny jumped at the sound of Lily's voice. "Sorry. Sort of got lost in thought there."

Lily set some fluffy white hand towels, a damp cloth, and some other items on the coffee table and sat down next to him. The other items included a bottle of hydrogen peroxide, a box of bandages, and a roll of tape. Her expression was neutral as she grabbed the damp cloth and looked at Johnny. "What were you thinking about?"

He shrugged and winced. "Lots of things."

She nodded noncommittally. "I'll bet. Now get that fucking shirt off before I have to tear it off you."

Now she smiled, raising an eyebrow in a speculative way.

Johnny frowned.

Oh, shit. Is she flirting with me?

Whatever else might happen from here on out, he knew he couldn't let things drift in that direction with her. Yes, there were some doubts where Nora was concerned, but one thing the events of the last couple days had driven home was that he was done pining for Lily. She was his past and he had to move forward without her. Whether that process included a life with Nora or something else was yet to be determined.

But Lily probably believed he harbored some leftover feelings she could exploit.

He would have to be careful.

He started to unbutton the Hawaiian shirt, but realized it was pointless. The shirt was ruined. He grabbed the front of it and ripped it open. Lily laughed as buttons went flying. Johnny tugged the bloody rag off and tossed it aside.

Lily winced as she peered at his wound. "Ouch. Looks worse than I thought."

"Thanks for the comforting words."

"Just telling it like it is, baby." She dabbed gently at the wound, rapidly cleaning away the majority of the blood even as more continued to trickle from the gash. She then took a folded-over hand towel and pressed it firmly against the wound, holding it down to soak up more of the blood. "I can only do so much for you. You're gonna need to get sewn up at the ER."

"What am I supposed to tell them about how this happened?"

Lily smirked. "Tell them the truth. Some plain Jane bitch attacked you with a knife."

"You're just being catty. Nora's pretty."

A corner of her mouth curled upward. "Compared to me?"

Johnny didn't say anything.

Lily laughed. "Your silence speaks volumes."

After a few minutes, Lily took the hand towel away and pronounced the blood flow sufficiently stanched. She splashed hydrogen peroxide on the wound and laughed when Johnny had to clamp down on a scream. She then applied a bandage after patting away the excess hydrogen peroxide.

"There. Not quite all better, but at least you're no longer bleeding like a stuck pig."

Instead of thanking her, Johnny blurted out a question he knew he should have kept to himself. "Why did you kill Jamie Benton?"

Surprise registered briefly on Lily's face, but it was gone so fast Johnny could almost believe he'd imagined it. "What makes you think I killed Jamie?"

Johnny swallowed and forced himself to stay calm and hold her gaze. He was suddenly very aware of the big knife lying within reach on the coffee table. "I was hiding in a closet at your place the day after it happened. I came by to check on you. I'd heard…something that led me to believe you might be in trouble."

Lily looked confused for a moment, but then awareness dawned and she smiled. "Nora told you about running into me at Kroger."

Johnny nodded. "Yeah."

"Meddling bitch."

Johnny ignored the comment. "Anyway, no one answered when I knocked. So I went around back and the door there was open."

Lily rolled her eyes. "Fucking Slick. Jesus. I don't know how many times we told him not to do that."

"I might have just given up, but your car was in the driveway and I was worried. I decided to let myself in and have a look around. When I found Jamie, I thought it was you. I was about to get the hell out of there when I heard voices. Hiding in the closet was my only option."

Lily watched Johnny closely, but she didn't say anything. She remained outwardly calm, but Johnny thought she seemed tenser now. He saw it in the slight narrowing of her eyes and in the almost imperceptible hardening of her jawline. He had an impulse to make a preemptive grab for the knife just to keep it away from her, but he thought that would escalate the situation in a way he still hoped would not be necessary.

"I stood in that closet and listened to your friends argue for what felt like forever. They were upset and panicking. I didn't know what to think at the time. In thinking about it now, my impression is of two people angry about having to do the hard work of covering up something done by another person. A person who was maybe too fucked up to help."

Lily's expression stayed blank a moment longer.

Then she laughed.

"Brilliant, Johnny. You missed your true calling in life, I think. You should have been a detective. Maybe your old pal Joe Voss could help you with that."

"Why did you kill Jamie Benton?"

"I was drunk. Honestly, I don't remember it very well. I do remember fighting with her and totally losing my shit." She shrugged. "I remember hitting her hard as I could over and over. And I remember her screaming and crying. But that's about it."

Johnny frowned. "Why were you fighting with her?"

"She made me mad, I guess."

"How did she make you mad?"

Lily sighed. "I've said all I have to say. Now you know who did what, more or less. That's enough."

She got to her feet and turned so she was facing him directly. She smiled as she pulled off her top and let it flutter to the floor.

Johnny sucked in a breath. "Lily--"

She kept smiling as she unhooked her bra and tossed it aside. "You were right before, you know. We know things about each other we don't want other people to know. And those secrets are safe because anything else means mutually assured destruction. So here's the deal, baby. As far as I'm concerned, we're back together. You can break it to that homely bitch tomorrow."

Johnny shook his head. "No."

But there wasn't much conviction in the utterance. He was too entranced by her nearly nude form, which he'd last glimpsed more than a year ago. Despite a slight coarsening that had occurred during that time as a result of her lifestyle, she retained much of her devastatingly erotic appeal. He knew he should know better—knew he should be issuing a firmer denial—but he just couldn't do it.

Lily's smile had a knowing quality to it. "You still want me. Anything else you've told yourself is a lie, a delusion. I'm tired of living in fucking squalor. I've had my little adventure and now I'm coming home. I'm sure you have doubts, but in time you'll be okay with this."

"No."

Lily wiggled out of her denim cutoffs and kicked them away.

She wasn't wearing panties.

Johnny had tremendous difficulty swallowing. His face turned bright red.

Lily started walking away from him, casting a last glance over her shoulder before she left the room. "I'll be in bed…waiting for you, Johnny."

And then she was gone from the room.

Johnny let out a huge breath and sagged against the back of the sofa. The clashing thoughts in his head reached a density approaching white noise. He could make no sense of anything. So he closed his eyes and did his damnedest to quiet the noise. It took several minutes, but he was finally able to do it.

He opened his eyes and stared numbly at the clutter of bloody items on the coffee table.

He knew what he had to do.

Johnny grabbed his keys and got out of the house.

25

A noise of some kind was buzzing somewhere in the vicinity of his right ear. A detached part of him understood there was a pattern to what he was hearing, a sequence of distinct sounds repeating over and over. The sequence was always the same, but the volume increased with each repetition, reflecting a growing agitation. Eventually he realized his name was a part of the sequence of sounds. The moment this insight penetrated, the rest of it snapped into jarringly clear focus.

A hand was on his shoulder. There was a tension in that grip. Slender fingers dug hard into his flesh. Good thing it wasn't the wounded shoulder or he'd be screaming by now. The grip was hard enough that it caused a dull pain, anyway. It hit Johnny that this was how you'd take hold of a person who needed shaking out of a stupor.

Johnny frowned.

Am I in a stupor?

A voice screamed in his ear: *"Johnny! Are you okay!?"*

Johnny cringed.

Not anymore, I'm not.

He glanced to his right and saw Madge Olson looking at him with obvious concern. Madge was a stout-bodied woman in her fifties with short gray hair and wire-rimmed glasses. She was a part-owner of Al's Cigar Boutique, the tobacco shop next to The Delirium Lounge. Al's was where Johnny went for all his smoking needs. A guy named Al was co-owner of the shop, but Al was never around for some reason. Johnny had long enjoyed kidding Madge about that, suggesting maybe she had offed Al at some point for reasons unknown and was just playing along with the assumption that the man was still alive.

Johnny didn't find the joke too funny anymore. It had never been a genuine rib-tickler, but recent developments in his life had robbed it of any meager humor it'd possessed.

He dragged on a cigarillo and blew out a little cloud of smoke. "I've had better days, Madge."

Madge relinquished her grip on him and climbed onto the stool next to him, thumping her purse down on the bar and digging out a pack of cigarettes. "You want to talk about it?"

Johnny dragged on the cigarillo again, exhaled another cloud of smoke. "I wouldn't want to make you an accessory after the fact. So…no."

She laughed. "That sounds serious."

Johnny shrugged and wedged the still-smoldering cigarillo into one of the rim notches of the ashtray in front of him. He picked up the tumbler of whiskey next to it and took a big sip. "I guess you could call it serious, yeah. But right now I'm trying hard not to think about it."

Madge sparked up a cigarette. "Have anything to do with the bitch who left you?"

Johnny drank some more whiskey and said nothing.

Madge laughed and dragged on the cigarette. "Say no more. I had my fill of listening to you cry about her a while ago. But you gotta tell me one thing, Johnny."

Johnny finished off the last of the whiskey in the tumbler. It was either his fifth or sixth double since arriving at the Delirium Lounge. He was getting to the point where he was starting to lose track. That was good. He wanted to lose himself tonight, in every possible sense. Oblivion was what he wanted. It reminded him of how he'd felt in those first terrible months after Lily left him. It was like getting reacquainted with an old and much-missed friend. His life now was dominated by darkness and confusion, as well as by the terrifying possibility of sudden, violent death. And he didn't know what to do about any of it—except to make it all go away for a while.

He shoved the empty tumbler across the bar. "What do you want to know, Madge?"

"What's the deal with the ridiculous shirt?"

Johnny groaned.

The fucking shirt. Jesus.

He'd fled his house without putting on a new shirt. This was partly the fault of the mental upheaval consuming him in those moments. There had been no thought given to anything other than getting the hell out of there. In a way, the oversight was a good thing. Changing into a new shirt at home would have meant going into the bedroom, which would have meant facing Lily again and that had been out of the question at the time.

Still, it had left him with a dilemma. He had wanted to go drink somewhere, preferably at one of his favorite public watering holes, but he couldn't have done so bare-chested with a big, bloody bandage strapped to his shoulder. So he had stopped off at a convenience store near his house to buy a T-shirt. Johnny wasn't a T-shirt guy by nature, but he couldn't very well go shopping for something decent in his current state. His options were limited and he figured any shirt that fit would do. So he grabbed a random XL off the rack without looking at it, tearing off the tag as he pulled it on. It fit well enough so he took the tag up to the counter and bought it, trying not to take the way the teenage clerk was stifling a giggle as she rang up his purchase personally.

The shirt was gray and had no image on it.

Emblazoned across the front in big block letters was a slogan—DON'T BE A RICHARD.

Johnny took a look at the front of his shirt and sighed.

Madge laughed. "Something tells me there's a hell of a story behind that."

Johnny grunted. "Yeah, it's a real ripsnorter."

"And that's all you intend to say on the subject, right?"

Johnny showed her a weary smile. "Sorry."

Mick was behind the bar tonight. There was a good crowd for the middle of the week and it took him a few minutes to make his way back over to where Johnny was sitting.. He gave Johnny a quizzical look and Johnny tilted his chin in the way that meant, "Hit me again."

Mick filled a fresh tumbler with Maker's Mark and pushed it across the bar to Johnny before shifting his attention to Madge. "I can't believe you let yourself be seen in public with this motherfucker," he said, jerking his head in Johnny's direction. "Think of your reputation, Madge."

Madge chuckled and puffed on her cigarette. "Fuck my reputation. Get me a Bloody Mary."

Mick laughed and started mixing her drink.

Johnny downed the glass of Maker's Mark like a shot. A tiny amount went down the wrong way and he almost choked on it. Somehow, though, he managed to avoid having to spew it all over the bar, which would have been embarrassing as hell. It also might have forced Mick to cut him off, which would have been even worse. Mick rarely ever had to shut Johnny down because he trusted him to always take an alternate way home if he got too sloppy. It was why Johnny came here so often. He could get his drink on without being hassled about being drunk.

But even Mick had his limits.

He eyed Johnny warily as he added the garnish to Madge's drink. "You okay, man? Your face is all red."

Johnny waved this away and pushed the empty glass across the bar. "I'm fine. Some of that just didn't go down right."

Mick nodded. "Drink the next one slower, okay?"

"You're the boss."

Johnny picked up the cigarillo and lit it again with the cheap plastic lighter he'd picked up at the same convenience store where he'd gotten the Richard shirt. In his haste to get out of his house, he'd also left behind his Zippo and cigarillos, which had been stashed in the breast pocket of the ruined Hawaiian shirt. The cigarillos he was smoking were also cheap re-placements, mass-produced crap rather than the quality hand-rolled smokes he bought from Madge. He didn't much care for the way they smelled or tasted, but they were better than noth-ing.

"I guess Riley's gone home for the day, huh?"

Mick handed Madge her drink and poured Maker's Mark for Johnny. A corner of his mouth twitched in a smirk. "Yeah, man, she took off a few hours ago."

He handed Johnny his drink.

Johnny frowned. "What's so funny?"

Mick shrugged, but that smirk was deepening. "She was talking about you before she left." He laughed. "Said you were, and I quote, 'cute for a geezer'."

Johnny picked up his drink. "Huh."

"She's half your age."

"Shit, I know that." Johnny said this with a tone of in-dignation he had to manufacture. "How dumb do you think I am?"

Mick cackled. "I don't know, Johnny. Pretty damn dumb sometimes."

"Fuck you."

Mick laughed and moved off to serve another customer.

The drinks kept coming and Johnny drifted in and out of conversations with Madge and other regulars. When his throat began to feel intolerably dry from all the smoking, he ordered a cold beer instead of another whiskey. Sometimes a beer hit the spot in just the right way. In this case, the bottle of Lagunitas IPA was so refreshing it was close to heavenly. He inhaled it inside of two minutes and immediately ordered another, which went down almost as fast. By the time he'd put away four beers, the world around him was swimming and he was having a hard time holding his head up. He tried to recall how many whiskey drinks he'd downed before starting in with the beer and found the answer elusive. Some would take this as a sign it was time to slow down or maybe even stop for the night, but for Johnny it only meant the oblivion he sought wasn't far away and obviously he had to keep drinking until he got there.

After one of his many stumbling trips to the bathroom to relieve his overburdened bladder, he returned to find his old buddy Joe Voss ensconced atop the barstool he'd vacated. This struck Johnny as an unacceptable violation of barroom ethics. The regulars at any given drinking joint knew not to pinch a pal's spot while he was off making room for more beer.

At least this was what Johnny told himself as he staggered back to the bar and slugged Voss in the shoulder. "Off my stool, you fucking cop bastard."

Voss swiveled away from Madge and gave Johnny his best hardass cop glare—a look that softened some when he got a look at who had slugged him. "Ah, shit. Johnny Doyle's on a tear." He frowned. "What's up with the shirt?"

Johnny scowled and repeated what he'd already said.

This earned a confused look from Voss. "I hate to break it to you, Richard, but I have no idea what you just said."

Johnny was about to repeat his demand that the off-duty cop remove his posterior from the spot that was rightfully his—possibly at a louder, more belligerent volume—when he realized he might be slurring his words enough to render them slightly unintelligible. So he paused a moment and when he spoke again, he put considerable effort into carefully enunciating each word. "Listen here, you goddamn seat-poaching, pig-fucking cocksucker. You need to get off that stool in about five seconds or there will be consequences."

This elicited belly-shaking laughter from Voss, who had to put down the bottle of Miller Lite he was holding lest the force of his mirth should cause him to spill it. After the laughing fit passed, he took a slug of beer and said, "Consequences, eh? What kind of consequences?"

"Fisticuffs."

Voss had the bottle raised to his mouth again. He put it down and gave his friend an incredulous look. "Fisticuffs? Seriously?"

Johnny nodded gravely. "Fisticuffs, motherfucker. This offense shall not stand. Offenses."

Now Voss looked even more confused. "There's more than one?"

Another nod from Johnny. "You called me Richard."

An acquaintance who happened to be walking by as Johnny said this glanced his way and said, "He called you a dick, basically, but only because you are one."

The acquaintance continued on past him—probably en route to the bathroom—chuckling in the wake of his hit-and-run comment. Johnny turned his head and shouted a reply: "I didn't need the goddamn clarification, asshole!"

Voss gave Johnny a long, appraising look. He appeared to be weighing whether this was good-natured joshing on Johnny's part or an actual threat. His expression was devoid of humor as he slipped back into cop mode. "Maybe you've had enough, Johnny. Let me call you a cab."

He put down his beer and picked up his cell phone.

Johnny barely resisted an urge to knock it out of his hand. But even through the fog of inebriation, he recognized this as an idea fraught with the potential for disaster. Recognizing this told Johnny he wasn't quite at the precipice of oblivion just yet, though what little sense of good judgment he still possessed was fragile at best. Joe Voss had been a good friend for a long time, but the man was a cop above all else. Antagonizing him too much would be a mistake, especially in his current condition.

He closed a hand around Voss's phone. "No cab. Not yet."

Voss squinted at him. "I'm serious, Johnny. You've had enough. And you're sure as hell not driving yourself home."

Johnny took out his wallet and put a hundred-dollar bill on the bar. He grabbed the pack of cheap cigarillos and the plastic lighter and gave Voss his most sincere look. "I won't drive, I promise, but I'm not going home yet. Gonna take a walk to clear my head."

He walked out of the Delirium Lounge before Voss could reply.

26

Outside on the sidewalk, Johnny fired up a cigarillo and puffed on it while he mulled over where to go next. He gave some brief thought to walking over to 3 Brothers, which was on the opposite side of the corner from the Delirium Lounge. It would be the easiest thing to do. He could be pounding beers again inside of a minute or so.

But the longer Johnny stood there and smoked, the less he felt inclined to act on the impulse. As usual, the square was lively at night. There was noise and music, people laughing. All at once, Johnny felt disconnected from his surroundings. His mood spiraled rapidly downward as the reason for tonight's descent into drunkenness was suddenly at the forefront of his consciousness again. He would resume his pursuit of oblivion as soon as possible. But this time he would do it in solitude. The desire to be around other people had vanished.

Johnny dropped the half-smoked cigarillo on the sidewalk and ground it out beneath the heel of his boot. After a glance at the dark-tinted windows of the Delirium Lounge, he dug his keys out of his hip pocket, got in the Austin-Healey, and backed out of his parking space. There was a squelch of tires behind him as another motorist slammed on the brakes to avoid hitting him. Johnny braked as well and glanced at his rearview mirror, glimpsing the front end of a Prius. He had missed hitting it by mere inches. The driver of the Prius shook a fist at him before driving on by.

This time he made sure the street behind him was clear before he finished backing out of the parking space and driving away from the Delirium Lounge. He did a jerky half-circuit of the roundabout—having to occasionally stomp on the brake pedal as young nighttime revelers wandered across the street with blithe disregard for vehicular traffic—before taking a side street away from the square.

He was able to breathe easier as soon as he was away from the noise and congestion. He felt more clear-headed and less prone to getting himself into trouble. Johnny knew this was mostly mental, but that was okay, because his mental state needed any kind of lift it could get.

The Austin-Healey swerved a little when he reached for the pack of cheap-ass cigarillos, causing him to temporarily forego his next nicotine fix. He gripped the wheel with both hands, opened his eyes wide, and focused all his energy on keeping the car between the yellow lines as he traveled north on Broad. He wasn't quite in what you could call full possession of his senses, but he wasn't yet far gone enough to make him unaware of how precarious his situation was. He was operating a vehicle while significantly impaired, which was both unlawful and extremely dangerous. Any cop who stopped him would haul his ass straight to jail.

Johnny knew what he was doing was stupid. He truly believed he was better at driving while buzzed than the average person, but he wasn't just buzzed. He was drunk. No way should he be driving. Someone could get hurt or killed. He might pass out behind the wheel and awake later to find he'd plowed into a station wagon, wiping out a family of six. Did people still drive station wagons? He wasn't sure. Anyway, obviously he didn't want to wipe out a station wagon family. Injuring himself would be okay, though. Right now he didn't much care about his personal safety. Death would be the ultimate form of oblivion, after all.

He was a bad person.

A killer. A corpse desecrator.

If he managed to kill himself through his own stupidity, it would be nothing less than what he deserved. Hurting someone else who just happened to be in the wrong place at the wrong time would be a fucking travesty. Maybe a swerve into the nearest utility pole would be the best solution all around. Not only would the motorists of Murfreesboro then be much safer, but Johnny Doyle would suddenly have a lot less stressful shit to deal with, being dead and all.

A part of him recognized the black train of thought for what it really was. Rather than bringing on oblivion, the alcohol was fueling a downward emotional spiral into melancholy and self-pity. Things might look more manageable—relatively speaking—if he could pull himself out of this tailspin and find somewhere quiet and dark to pull over and sober up. However, the part of him that wanted only to keep drinking dismissed this as proof positive that he wasn't nearly drunk enough yet.

Johnny gave the wheel of the Austin-Healey a hard jerk to the right when he spied the bright lights of a convenience store coming up fast on that side of the road. He aimed for the entrance to the parking lot, but missed it and wound up bouncing over the curb. His seatbelt wasn't on and his head struck the roof of the car with some force.

He grimaced. "Ouch."

By some miracle, he managed to keep the car under control and pulled into a parking space that was the farthest removed from the store's entrance. He shut off the engine, but did not immediately get out of the car. Instead he checked his reflection in the rearview mirror and winced at the sight of how florid his face looked. The redness in his eyes was also telling. There could be no deceiving himself—he looked like a drunk, probably smelled like one, too.

Johnny thought about searching his glovebox for a pack of chewing gum but choose not to upon instantly realizing two things.

One, no amount of gum could obscure the overpowering reek of booze currently wafting out of his pie-hole.

And two, he didn't chew gum.

Also, addendum to points one and two—*Fuck it.*

Johnny got out of the Austin-Healey and took a moment to make sure he had his balance before stepping up onto the sidewalk and approaching the store's entrance with careful, deliberate steps. The world did a lot less spinning than he'd anticipated and he began to suspect his concerns about impairment had been unfounded.

But then his left foot slid off the edge of the sidewalk and he took a painful tumble to the asphalt, bruising bones and scraping flesh in the process.

He looked up at the dark sky and sighed. "Well, shit."

There was one thing to be grateful for, at least—no one else was in the parking lot. It was a minor miracle, but he knew he wouldn't have the lot to himself for long. He needed to haul himself up off his drunk ass before a cop or someone else came along. Grunting with exertion—and making his face redder than ever, he suspected—he managed to get it done. He thought it likely someone in the store had observed the tumble. That no one had come rushing to his aid was unsurprising. Convenience store employees—particularly those working the night shift—typically weren't inclined to rush to the aid of a drunken, odiferous bum, which was no doubt exactly what he resembled. Hell, they were more apt to chase off such people and threaten to call the police.

All things considered, his best course here might be to return to the car and call someone to come pick him up. The Austin-Healey could be retrieved tomorrow, when he was sober again. But the question of who to call perplexed him. He sure as shit couldn't call Joe Voss. For one thing, the guy would be pissed that Johnny had lied to him about not driving. He might even drag him off to jail just to teach him a lesson. He doubted Nora would even answer a call from him right now. He wanted to fix things with her, but it would have to wait for another time, given his advanced state of inebriation.

Johnny had a hunch Lily wouldn't hesitate to come get him. Hell, she'd probably get here in record time. But he wouldn't be calling her, either. For one thing, he didn't want to set a precedent of turning to her when he was in trouble. Even the slightest step in that direction would be dangerous. Given the events of the day, he'd have to deal with her again soon enough, but it didn't need to be now.

A glare of headlights as a car turned into the convenience store's parking lot made Johnny squint and sway on his feet. The headlights slid away from him as the car pulled up at a gas pump. Loud music thumped from the car's speakers. It was something modern with a lot of bass and synthesizer. The car was a Taurus with tinted windows. It had custom chrome hub-caps and flame decals on the doors. The decals struck Johnny as apt. He was sure there was zero chance of anyone in the Taurus being anything other than a flaming douchebag.

Johnny had an urge to get in the Austin-Healey and take his chances on the road. Nothing good could come of interacting with whoever was in the Taurus. But then he thought of how badly he wanted another drink. All he had to do here was keep his head down and not engage anyone long enough to purchase some beer and be on his way.

How difficult could that be?

The Middle Eastern man behind the counter eyed Johnny warily as he came into the store. Johnny nodded at him before threading his way through the aisles to the back of the store, where he ducked into the public restroom to take a piss. He nearly took another tumble when he lifted the dirty toilet lid with the toe of his boot, but he managed to stay upright and get the fly of his jeans unzipped. He groaned as he unleashed a jet-propelled stream of urine, not all of which went into the bowl. His unsteadiness made hitting the target problematic. A lot of it splashed against the rim and some drops even hit the floor. Johnny had to laugh. This was precisely why convenience store restrooms were often so foul—all the drunks coming in to piss.

When he was done, he washed his hands and ripped paper towels from a dispenser mounted on the wall. As he dried his hands, he heard multiple loud voices out in the store. There were male and female voices. They all sounded young. One of the guys was braying obnoxious laughter at someone else's every utterance.

Johnny was tempted to remain in the bathroom until they were gone from the store. Though most of his current-day acquaintances didn't know him as a brawler, there had been some incidents in his youth, almost all of which had involved too much booze and situations just like this one, in which he found himself mixing it up with obnoxious, loudmouthed cretins. Sometimes he had come out on top in those situations and sometimes he had not, but always he'd lived to fight another day. Back then he'd had youth and vigor on his side. Now he was a middle-aged guy in questionable shape. Responding to any kind of provocation would likely result in getting his ass severely beaten. So, yeah, staying right here a few minutes longer was the smart way to go.

But some of the loud voices came uncomfortably close to the bathroom. The doorknob jiggled as someone tried it and found it locked. Then the door shook in the frame as someone pounded on it. Johnny winced. Instantly pounding on the door of a public restroom upon finding it locked was yet another reliable douchebag indicator. This situation was looking grimmer all the time.

Well, standing in here while the person on the other side of the door got more and more belligerent wouldn't help matters any. Johnny dropped the damp paper towels on top of an overflowing trash can and opened the door. He was scarcely out the door before a scowling, muscular young guy in a golf shirt and khaki shorts barged his way past Johnny into the restroom. The guy shouted at him from behind the door when it was closed again: *"Took you long enough, motherfucker!"*

Johnny stared at the door and frowned.

"You mad, bro?"

Johnny glanced to his left. Another muscular frat boy type in a golf shirt was smirking at him. Two girls were with him. Both were shapely blondes with fake tans and skimpy attire. One had a septum piercing and some lame tribal tattoos. She probably thought the tattoos and the piercing made her look edgy.

He moved away from the restroom and approached the nearest beer cooler.

The other frat guy turned as he tracked Johnny's movements. "You look mad."

Johnny opened the cooler and took out a six-pack of Bud tall boys. Far from what he would usually choose for himself, but it would do for now. It had alcohol in it. That was all that mattered. He let the cooler's door flap shut and started toward the checkout counter.

He was unsurprised when the asshole followed him. At this point, the real surprise would have been the guy taking any other action.

A finger poked at his back as he set the six-pack on the counter.

"Look at me, bro."

The clerk rang up the purchase and Johnny tossed a twenty on the counter. He had a feeling the clerk would have given him grief about his intoxicated state if not for the frat guy's belligerence. The poor clerk obviously wanted only to speed along the transaction and get Johnny out of the store before the situation could escalate. Johnny's goal was the same, so he just stood there while the clerk hurriedly made change.

The frat guy poked his back again. "It's rude not to answer when someone asks you a question, bro."

Johnny took his change and pushed it into a pocket. He pried one of the tall cans from the plastic ring-binder, gave it several hard shakes, and turned around to face the jackass. "I'm not your bro."

He popped the tab on the can and aimed the opening at the frat guy's smirking face. An explosion of fizzy foam wiped the smirk away and sent him staggering backward, crashing into a snack food display. Twinkies, snack cakes, and frosted cinnamon buns went flying and got trampled as the guy struggled to keep his footing.

Shit. So much for keeping my head down.

The girls were shrieking and one of them was repeatedly calling out for someone named Kyle, who had to be the guy in the restroom. The accuracy of this guess was verified seconds later when the restroom door flew open and he came storming through the aisles to see what was going on. Kyle's first reaction when he saw his buddy's beer-drenched face and shirt was a bark of laughter. He then noticed that everyone's attention was focused on Johnny and suddenly he was sneering again.

He took some menacing steps in Johnny's direction. "The fuck did you do, asshole?"

"You need to beat the shit out of him."

This was the girl with the septum piercing.

Kyle glanced at her. "What did this motherfucker do?"

She smiled as she looked right at Johnny. "He shook up one of his beers and sprayed it in Ethan's face. For no good reason."

Kyle curled his hands into fists and took another step toward Johnny. "Is that right?"

The girl with the septum piercing nodded. "It was totally unprovoked."

Johnny sighed.

It was one of the most bald-faced lies he'd ever heard. The clerk could attest to the very real provocation that had occurred, but he was too busy yelling at them all to get the hell out of his store. There was little point in trying to refute the girl's absurdly malicious claim.

Johnny grabbed the rest of his beers and walked out of the store. He was more than halfway to the Austin-Healey when he heard the store's door bang open behind him. His stomach knotted at the sound. For a moment he'd believed he might avoid any repercussions for his rash act if he could just move fast enough. Once he was safely inside his car there would be nothing they could do.

"Where do you think you're going, asshole?"

Johnny cursed himself for parking at the far end of the lot. The Austin-Healey was still a good half-dozen or more long strides away and they were right behind him. Escape wasn't possible. That being the case, there was no use in letting them chase him down like a dog.

He pried another beer from the plastic ring-binder. He pivoted and cocked an arm back like a shortstop making a throw to first base. There was just enough time to draw a rough bead on the closest of the frat thugs. He then whipped his arm forward and the tall can sliced through the crisp night air. It happened fast, but for Johnny there was a perfect frozen moment of seeing the can in mid-flight juxtaposed against the startled faces of Ethan and Kyle, who were too close to get out of the way or otherwise react. It was an image he knew would stay with him the rest of his life, which might only amount to a few more minutes. The can hit Kyle's face dead-center, breaking his nose with an audible snap. Johnny felt a moment of wild triumph as the antagonistic muscle-head went reeling backward.

The moment was short-lived.

Ethan let out a shriek of rage and pounced. The rest of Johnny's beers went flying as the large man tackled him. He hit the asphalt with a painful thud. Ethan's fists felt hard as bricks. They made cracking sounds as they crashed against Johnny's face. A tooth got jarred loose and he somehow managed to spit it out even as Ethan continued to pummel him. There was a brief respite as Ethan was pulled away by Kyle, who wanted a shot at Johnny for breaking his nose. If anything, Kyle hit even harder than his friend. They were quite the goddamn tag team. The pain was tremendous, mitigated only slightly by Johnny's high blood alcohol level.

But Kyle had only managed to land a couple blows by the time the Middle Eastern clerk came out of the store and fired a gun into the air. The loud bang elicited startled shrieks from the girls. Then the clerk was yelling at them, telling them he'd called 911 and the police were on the way. For Johnny this was a case of good news and bad news. The good news was the beating had come to an abrupt end. His face felt swollen and sore, but he was alive and had suffered no damage from which he couldn't recover. The bad news was the impending arrival of the police. He had no more interest in facing them than the frat thugs did.

The bulk of the asshole brigade made an immediate break for the Taurus. Johnny had just heaved a sigh of relief when he heard of click of heels and saw the girl with the septum piercing standing over him. She smiled. Perplexed, Johnny smiled back. A part of him realized there was no good reason to smile. It was nothing but reflex. He couldn't understand why she was lingering over him while her friends were busy fleeing. Her friends evidently couldn't figure it out either, because within seconds they were screaming at her, urging her to stop fucking around and get in the car. The store clerk was doing some more yelling of his own. He was spewing a lot of barely intelligible threats, most of them involving the police.

Then the girl with the septum piercing stepped on his outstretched hand and ground it beneath the heel of her shoe. She bit down on her bottom lip and put all her weight into it. Johnny heard bones crunching and squealed in agony.

She dropped her voice to a level too low to be heard by anyone other than Johnny and said, "That's for being such a fucking Richard."

She squawked laughter.

Then she was gone, her heels clicking rapidly on asphalt.

Johnny groaned.

Goddamn shirt. Fucking hell.

One of the sadistic girl's friends shouted something at her, a shrill expression of frustrated rage and fear. A moment later, doors thunked shut and the Taurus went screeching out of the parking lot. As it sped away, a feminine voice screamed out a single word: *"Richard!"*

Johnny groaned and closed his eyes as he allowed his head to settle against the warm asphalt. The immediate threat was gone, but the intensity of the pain inflicted by his assailants had not faded. If anything, it was burning brighter than ever.

He winced and opened his eyes as he felt the toe of someone's shoe nudge his ribs. The store clerk was standing over him. He had a phone in one hand and the gun he'd used to scare away the college kids in the other. Johnny squinted at the gun and almost laughed in spite of the pain. The gun was a starter pistol. It looked very much like the real thing but had an orange plug in the barrel. It only fired blanks. Johnny didn't know what good such a thing would do when aimed directly at a would-be robber—unless he was blind—but in this case it had done the job. Maybe the clerk only kept it around specifically for situations like this one.

The clerk's look of wild-eyed indignation had vanished. In its place was what looked like actual sympathy. "Cops will be here in a minute." The man spoke with only the slightest trace of an accent. "Maybe you should go."

Johnny nodded and sat up. He cast a look around him and spotted two of the tall Bud cans. One was wedged beneath one of the Austin-Healey's rear tires and the other was within grabbing distance. He retrieved both, dug out his keys, and got in the Austin-Healey.

Moments later he was speeding away from the convenience store. Just in the nick of time, too, because he'd only gotten a quarter mile down the road by the time he saw flashing patrol car lights go racing by in the opposite direction. Worried that the cop might double back and try to catch up to him after arriving at the convenience store and finding the troublemakers gone, he took a right at the next side street he came to and hit the gas. A couple minutes later he turned down another side street. This one led him to Memorial Boulevard, a wide thoroughfare that would eventually take him back to his neighborhood.

Johnny sighed in relief and popped the tab on one of the tall Bud cans.

It sprayed fizz in his face.

Johnny laughed.

He thought it was to his credit that he only swerved slightly when this happened. A glance at his rearview mirror showed that he'd yet again evaded being popped by the police for reckless driving. Maybe his luck was finally changing for the better. He blew foam off the top of the can and took a long swallow from it.

The sixteen-ounce can was empty when he turned down the street leading to his house. He crumpled it and tossed it in the back, reaching immediately for the sole remaining can. It rolled away from him on the shotgun seat and he had to strain for it. His fingers had just curled around slick aluminum made moist by condensation when he realized he was about to pass his driveway. Rather than stepping on the brake, he let go of the can, leaned back in the other direction, and cranked the steering wheel hard enough to take a sharp turn into the driveway. The Austin-Healey shot by Nora's Mercedes and slammed into the closed garage door. A last second stomp on the brake pedal was the only thing that prevented total disaster. However, the impact was hard enough to severely dent the garage door, and one of the car's headlights immediately stopped functioning.

The impact had also thrown Johnny against the steering wheel. The pain this caused wasn't much compared to what he had already endured tonight. He let out a wheezing breath as he fell back against the seat and waited to see if Lily or one of the neighbors would come out to check on the commotion.

Several minutes passed.

No one came out to investigate.

This struck Johnny as passing strange, but he wasn't about to complain. He was just grateful he wouldn't have to explain the damage until later. When he was certain his noisy return had passed unnoted, he backed the car up and parked it properly. He then stared at the big dent in the garage door and shook his head, realizing that if it looked bad in the dark, it would look far worse in the light of day. The damage to his car was probably at least as ugly. It pained him to think of it. Getting a vintage ride like the Austin-Healey repaired would cost a pretty penny. He would pay whatever it took, of course, but not without cringing.

Johnny hunted down the last Bud can—which had gone flying in the collision with the garage door—and found it lodged beneath the shotgun seat. He tapped the top of the can several times before opening it to blunt the unavoidable burst of foam. Foam rushed from the opening when he popped the tab, but it didn't explode in his face. Johnny blew the foam away and chugged down his last beer. He felt sad for a moment until he remembered there was loads more alcohol in the house.

He would dip into his personal booze supply soon enough, but he opted to remain where he was a few moments longer first, shaking his head as he reflected on the events of the night. It was fair to say he had behaved stupidly at virtually every point along the way. He touched his sore jaw and winced. Then he looked at the bright red spot in the center of his palm where the girl's heel had ground into it. The sharp edges of the heel had abraded the flesh, creating little tufts of torn skin. He thought of the way she'd looked at him while doing it, how she'd obviously derived joy from causing him pain.

Lately his life was full of people who wanted to hurt him.

Even goddamn strangers.

He thought again of how none of the problems currently facing him would even be an issue if he'd just minded his own damn business the other day.

He smacked the base of a fist against the steering wheel.

Stupid. Fucking stupid.

Unfortunately, he couldn't take back any of his stupid decisions. He would just have to cope with the consequences and figure out how to move forward. But that was something that could wait for daylight and sobriety.

For now...

Johnny got out of the Austin-Healey and swayed on his feet as he lurched in the direction of the sidewalk. Halfway to the porch he realized he'd left the car's door open. He turned around and started back toward the car. After a few steps, he stumbled and wound up face-down in the yard. He was losing track of how many times he'd fallen tonight, which was a bad fucking sign. Or a good one, from a seeking oblivion point of view.

He got up and staggered over to his car.

After he got the door shut, he took a moment to make sure he had his balance and started back down the sidewalk. In a few moments he was inside his house. He kicked the door shut and groped for the light switch. He found it and flipped it up, squinting against the glare. There was something off about the foyer and it took him a few moments to realize someone had swept up the remnants of the shattered vase.

Lily, of course.

Who else?

He wobbled into the living room and saw she had cleaned up in there, too. She had been busy in his absence. He guessed she'd done it either out of boredom or in an attempt to make a good impression. The latter made more sense. He figured she was sincere in her desire to come back, at least for a while. No way could he let her come back for real, but she no doubt was convinced she had the necessary leverage to make it happen.

Well, they'd just have to see about that.

Johnny went into the kitchen.

The bottle of Knob Creek was still on the counter. He grabbed it and spun the cap off. His fumbling fingers couldn't hold onto the cap and it fell to the floor. Fuck it. He wouldn't need it again anyway. He put the bottle to his mouth and drank deeply from it. He sighed in deep satisfaction, savoring the whiskey's sweet burn after the influx of too much fizzy cheap beer. He took another deep slug and started to feel a smidge better. He would be stiff and sore tomorrow—and possibly full of a bunch of new regrets—but for now he was kind of okay.

His stomach growled. He was even feeling a little peck-ish, apparently.

Johnny went to his fridge and pulled open the door. The bottle of Knob Creek slipped from his fingers and shattered on the floor. Because that was when he realized Lily had not been responsible for the cleanup efforts evident in the other rooms.

Someone had pulled out all the food and drink items.

In their place—numerous plastic-wrapped body parts.

Lily's face stared out at him from behind a multiple-thickness of stretchy plastic wrap, the kind used for sealing up leftovers or grocery store meat. The rest of her had been cut up into many little pieces. The pieces were crammed in on the shelves and in the side slots on the doors. Every available space was filled with Lily.

Johnny initially just stood there and stared at her for several minutes. He was too drunk to make any kind of sense of what he was seeing. Sober, the shock of it would have been instantaneous. He might even have run screaming from the house. But he was fucked up and he was having great difficulty comprehending the gruesome reality before him.

Finally, however, he'd stood there long enough for it to penetrate.

Johnny screamed and backed away from the fridge, his boots crunching on shards of the broken whiskey bottle. The fridge door closed when he let go of it, mercifully taking away the grisly vision. His mind roiled with a thousand half-formed thoughts and possibilities, none of which he could even begin to get a handle on out of a combination of shock and alcohol intoxication.

His stomach fluttered and bile rose into his throat. He gagged as he choked it down and reeled out of the kitchen. An attack of extreme lightheadedness made everything go gray for a moment. When clarity returned, he was in the hallway leading to the bedroom, bracing his hands on the walls as he lurched from side to side. By the time he reached the bedroom, his stomach was in full revolt. He ran to the bathroom, desperation propelling him forward despite the way his legs wanted to give out.

He didn't quite make it to the toilet. A spasm of intense nausea dropped him to his knees and he sprayed vomit on the white floor tiles. His throat throbbed and his stomach kept convulsing. This bout of sickness wasn't anywhere close to over. He got himself moving toward the toilet, his arms shaking as he dragged his hands through the puddle of puke.

Johnny flipped up the toilet seat and the next blast went into the bowl.

He was sick for a long while.

Once the last spasms of nausea had passed, he fell away from the toilet and rolled onto his side, curling into a fetal position as he shivered and moaned on the floor. He blanked his mind and tried hard not to think about what he had seen in the kitchen. Doing so would only invite another wave of painful dry heaves.

After a while, his eyes fluttered and began to close.

In his last moments of consciousness, a disturbing thought flitted through his tortured mind—*Nora's car…in the driveway…*

How the hell had he overlooked the potential significance of that little fact?

It was a question he would have to ponder at a later time.

Johnny Doyle passed out.

27

Many hours passed before he returned to consciousness. This was clear from the bright morning sunlight filtering through the half-closed shutters over the bathroom window. The inside of his mouth felt like dirty sandpaper, dry and gritty and tainted by the lingering taste of bile. His body remained locked in the fetal position. He felt like something that had shriveled up and died only to somehow be miraculously restored to life. A massive hangover ache made his head throb to the point of total distraction. Dealing with the wild array of problems facing him didn't seem possible. It was a process that couldn't even begin unless he was first able to address two overwhelming needs—painkillers and water, and huge quantities of each.

After hacking up and expelling some phlegm, he pulled his arms away from his chest and reached for the toilet seat above him. At the same time, he began to stretch out his legs. His joints creaked with the effort. It was like trying to make decades-old machinery start working again after a long period of disuse. What he needed was some goddamn WD-40 for his fucking knees. Stiff joints had plagued him since the onset of middle-age, but this was ridiculous. It was like he'd aged thirty more years overnight.

Fucking alcohol. I'll never drink again.

Johnny imagined he could hear the devil's faint, mocking laughter. The vow to never drink again was one the infernal bastard had heard countless times. They both knew only death would finally quench his thirst.

167

He clamped a hand tight around the edge of the toilet seat and began to haul himself up. This was how hard shit got done, by taking one little step at a time, one after another, until the task was accomplished. The effort was causing him much pain, and each little moment felt more like a thousand years, but he knew this was only the faulty perception of an anguished mind. He had to stay focused on the reality behind the perception. In just a few more moments, he would be on his feet. And then he would be at the sink, washing down painkillers with glass after glass of refreshing water.

His other hand closed around the toilet seat.

He was up on one knee now. Huffing and puffing, but making progress.

Come on, he thought. *Keep going. One goddamn step at a time.*

He let out a breath and began to pull his other knee upward. And that was when a monster cramp seized the muscles in his lower leg. He howled in pain and let go of the toilet seat, falling onto his side as he hit the floor again. He grabbed at his leg and mewled miserably, several minutes passing before the muscles even started to relax. Even then it was several more minutes before the cramp finally released him. When it did, he sobbed in relief and stayed where he was a while longer before making another attempt to get off the floor.

Johnny had suffered cramps similar to this one a handful of times. They always followed on the heels of an especially epic drinking episode. The cause was severe dehydration. Past experience had taught him to always down a tall glass of water before crashing for the night after a long bout of boozing. It was a usually reliable way of staving off this kind of thing. But last night he hadn't been thinking straight. He'd been too distraught to follow the usual procedure, too overcome with the horror of...

Holy shit. Lily...

That moment was the first time he'd thought of her since regaining consciousness. The horror of seeing her plastic-wrapped face staring out at him from his refrigerator hit him with enervating force. He was shaking again and felt like throwing up, but there was nothing of real substance left in his stomach to expel. An attack of dry heaves would only scald his throat with stomach acids. So he took some slow, deep breaths and tried hard to control his gag reflex.

After a while, it began to work and he was able to think about what he'd seen the previous night without becoming queasy. He tried telling himself it hadn't really happened, that what he was "remembering" was actually a vivid fragment from some terrible, deeply fucked-up dream, the kind he often had after a night of overindulgence. It was a plausible scenario, but he didn't really believe it.

There had been many times when he'd downed enough booze to blot out memories or make what memories he had unreliable, but last night had not been one of those times. The physical problems he was experiencing were a result of carelessness as much as anything else. His memories of all that had happened were quite clear.

A fact that led to an inevitable question—what crazy, sick fuck had killed Lily and stuffed the chopped-up pieces of her body in his refrigerator?

Nora was the first suspect that came to mind. She had already expressed a willingness to kill Lily. He had a hard time imagining Nora perpetrating the act in so gruesome a way, but perhaps the embarrassment of being temporarily banished from his house had sent her over the edge. Slick was dead and the only other people with even a remote connection to the situation were Barry Miller and Bree Sloan. Miller was a guy who dealt in death for a living and was accustomed to handling corpses. Maybe he had dismembered Lily at Nora's bidding, perhaps in exchange for more sexual favors. But then why wrap the body parts in plastic and leave them in his refrigerator? That touch strongly suggested the work of a disturbed mind. Obviously they had been left on display as a way of taunting and tormenting him.

Johnny didn't know much about Bree Sloan, but he did know she had a volatile personality. Whether she was unbalanced enough to butcher Lily, however, he didn't know.

Only one thing was certain—the answers to these questions wouldn't be discovered by continuing to lie on the bathroom floor. Yes, his last attempt to get up hadn't gone well, but that wasn't a good enough excuse for continued inaction. There was work to be done and a course of action to be determined. The situation was probably hopeless, but until he was dead or in jail giving up was not an acceptable option.

Johnny rolled onto his stomach, braced his hands on the cool floor tiles, and surged to his feet with a loud grunt of exertion. Doing it fast and bulling his way through the pain was the only way to make it happen. The effort was successful, but his right leg's calf muscles remained tender in the aftermath of the savage cramp. He limped his way to the sink, keeping as much weight as he could off the gimpy leg. At the sink, he turned on the cold water tap and filled a paper cup from the wall dispenser. He drank it down, filled the cup again, and opened the medicine cabinet above the sink. He shook several pills out of a bottle and washed them down with the second cup of water.

After gulping down several more cups of water, he limped back over to the toilet to take a piss. While he was relieving himself, he happened to glance in the direction of the open bathroom door and frowned. Something was off-kilter and it took him a few moments to figure out what it was. The reason he couldn't figure out the nature of that off-kilter something was because everything looked so normal. But then it hit him that the normality itself was the problem. He'd sprayed puke all over the floor prior to passing out, but now there was nary a hint of the mess.

A deep crease formed in the middle of his brow.

What the fuck?

For a moment he thought maybe he *had* dreamed all of it. It was a lovely, hopeful feeling, but one he was only able to take seriously for a few seconds. Nothing could erase the reality of having awakened next to the toilet. He had come in here and puked his guts out, making a hell of a mess in the process. That much he knew for a damn fact. But who had cleaned up after him? And why?

The killer had done it.

Who else?

The thought sent a shiver of fear down his spine. He imagined the murderer walking in here with a mop and a bucket, maybe whistling a jaunty tune as he or she cleaned up Johnny's puddles of sick—all while he was zonked out on the floor. It was an odd and unnerving mental image. He couldn't imagine why a deranged murderer would do such a thing.

Unless...

Well, unless the killer was toying with him. Wasn't that the sort of thing the really crazy types did sometimes? Sure, they liked to play sick little mind games and prolong the thrill of the whole thing. He could see Bree Sloan being into that kind of thing.

Johnny thought of the gun in his safe. He'd locked it up again after shooting Slick. Maybe his next move ought to be getting to it as soon as possible. Just in case. The safe was buried under books and the remains of a shattered bookcase, but he should be able to get to it easily enough. The longer he thought about it, the more he realized it was the only next step that made sense. Everything else could wait until he had the gun in hand.

He left the bathroom as stealthily as he could manage, treading as lightly as possible on the bedroom floor. But he was still limping, which made noiseless movement impossible. The floorboards creaked beneath him with each thumping stride of his stronger left leg. His heart was pounding as he reached the bedroom door and peered out into the short hallway.

He let out a breath.

The hallway was empty.

He slipped out of the bedroom and hop-skipped down the hallway until he reached an archway on the left. Through the archway was a longer hallway that led to the office. He wasn't looking forward to sifting through the mess to get to the safe—it would mean getting down on his knees again after fighting so hard to get upright, for one thing—but he needed to feel that gun in his hand before he could even think about doing anything else.

Johnny entered his office.

And stood just inside the door with his mouth open in surprise.

Okay, seriously, what in the name of blue fucking hell is going on here?

Whoever had cleaned up the mess in the bathroom had also been busy in here. The bullet-riddled bookcase was gone. The spilled books were arranged in neat stacks in a corner of the room. The heavy steel safe now sat next to the stereo receiver on the table behind his desk. Johnny shook off his shock and hurried over to it. He worked the combination dial and had the safe's door open inside of a few seconds. A wave of relief swept through him when he saw that the gun and the cash were still inside.

He took out the gun and walked out of the office. His right leg was feeling steadier beneath him as he continued back down the hallway. That was something, at least. Maybe it wouldn't be totally useless in the event of a struggle. When he reached the foyer, He peeked out a window and saw that Nora's Mercedes was no longer in the driveway.

His next stop was the kitchen. The broken whiskey bottle shards were gone. By now this wasn't a surprise, but it was no less troubling for that.

Johnny stood in front of the refrigerator and stared at the closed door.

His fingers clenched around the grip of the gun as he again summoned the image of what he'd seen last night. Just the thought of it set his heart to pounding again. His breath was coming out in gasps and he felt a tickle of nausea. He was in no hurry to have another look at the sickening thing that had been done to Lily. But that was the thing. He could no longer be sure she was still in there. In fact, she probably wasn't. For whatever reason, someone had put significant effort into covering up any hint of anything amiss having occurred.

He grabbed the door and yanked it open.

He immediately let it swing shut again.

Lily was still in there.

Her head—which originally had been placed in an upright position on the shelf—had fallen onto its side, but her face had looked out at him, her mouth open in a frozen scream. Though the body parts had been stored in the fridge, a mild death smell had wafted out when he'd opened the door. The odor wasn't as bad as it would have been if the remains had been left out to turn room temperature ripe, but freezing her would have been more effective.

Johnny's eyes flicked up to look at the freezer door.

Don't do it.

Johnny grimaced. "Shit."

He had to know.

He opened the freezer door and saw plastic-wrapped hands and feet. Lily's scarlet-painted nails looked somehow too bright protruding from the pale, frozen digits. Like the refrigerator's main compartment, the freezer had been emptied of all the food items it'd contained, chiefly a bunch of unhealthy microwave dinners.

Johnny closed the freezer door.

He backed away from the refrigerator and stood in the center of the kitchen while he wondered what he should do next. But then it came to him. It was so obvious it stunned him he hadn't thought of it right away. He had to get out of the damn house and take Lily with him. Just put her in a box or something—he was sure he had something suitable out in the junk-cluttered garage—and cart her out to the countryside. There he could burn the remains and bury them deep. It would be an awful fucking thing, but it would be a damn sight better than leaving her in his house. He couldn't imagine why her killer had left her here after doing such a stellar cleanup just with the rest of it and he didn't care.

He just wanted her gone.

In another moment he would have headed to the garage to begin his preparations.

But that was when he heard the front door creak open.

And then the voice, calling out to him: "Johnny? Are you in here? You shouldn't leave your front door unlocked, man. This town's not as safe as it used to be."

The hardwood floor creaked as Joe Voss entered the living room.

The voice called out to him again: "Answer if you can hear me, Johnny. That's a pretty big dent you put in your garage door, pal. How many times have I warned you about the drinking and driving? One of these days you're gonna get yourself killed, you know."

More creaking footsteps.

"I know I'm sort of butting in where I'm not wanted, but I'm worried about you, buddy. And I'm only here because Nora called and said you had some leftovers I should try."

Johnny couldn't help it.

He laughed.

28

Night had fallen by the time Johnny knocked on Nora's front door. She had a smug look on her face when she opened it moments later. Her hair was arranged in a stylish updo and she stood barefoot in a strappy little blue dress, the hem of which hit at mid-thigh and showed off her shapely legs. A nearly empty wine glass was clasped lightly in an upraised hand. After giving him a smirking once-over, she stepped back and invited him in with a tilt of her chin.

Johnny entered the house.

Nora shut the door and led the way to her living room, which was smaller than the living room in Johnny's house. It also had a cozier, more lived-in feel. The décor was tasteful and the furniture had a thrift-store vintage look, which was a false impression. The pieces had all been purchased new from high-end specialty retailers and looked more authentically vintage than real secondhand crap. The muted lighting aided the impression. Nora's living room was lit only by low-wattage bulbs in floor lamps.

She waved a hand at a red crushed velour sofa. "Have a seat. I'll get you a drink. What will you have?"

Johnny sat. "Beer, please."

Nora smirked again. "Taking it easy after last night, then? Smart boy."

She walked out of the room before he could reply. Johnny sat there and drummed his fingers on the knees of his black jeans. He had been anticipating this confrontation with Nora all day, wondering how she'd play it and whether she'd even let him through the door. In her place, he would have cut off all contact and might even have opted to stay somewhere else for a while. But Nota was a picture of perfect composure, appearing utterly unfazed by either Johnny's unannounced appearance at her house or any of the wild events of the last two days. In retrospect, it was what he should have expected. With the exception of her angry reaction to his rejection of her murder scheme, it was how she had been every step of the way.

Johnny glanced at his watch and frowned.

Five minutes had passed.

Grabbing a beer from the kitchen shouldn't take so long. For that matter, he'd heard no sounds emanating from the kitchen the entire time she'd been gone. There should have been a clinking of glass or the sound of a refrigerator door opening and closing.

But there was nothing.

Just perfect silence.

Johnny tugged at the bill of his black baseball cap, wedging it more firmly into place. He had tied his hair back with a rubber band and had tucked it under the cap, which kept trying to slide off his head. Once he was sure it was sufficiently locked down, he scooted to the edge of the sofa and glanced in the direction of the kitchen, a small section of which was visible through a high, curved archway.

If she didn't come out of there in about two minutes—

The thought was interrupted when she came waltzing through the archway with a dripping-wet bottle of Stella Artois in one hand and her cell phone in the other. She smiled when she caught Johnny's eye. "I hope you don't mind. I slipped out to the deck a minute to have a private chat with Barry."

She sat next to him on the sofa and handed him the beer. He took a small sip from the bottle and eyed her speculatively. "Oh? What about?"

She laughed. "Oh, please. You know why."

Johnny nodded. "He helped you, didn't he? With cleaning up and with what you did to Lily."

Nora smiled. "Before I say anything else, I need you to take off your clothes."

"No offense, but I'm not in the mood."

Nora rolled her eyes and her smile faded. "Nor am I, Johnny. I think we've been intimate for the last time, to tell you the truth. Oh, my. You almost look hurt. It shouldn't come as a surprise, baby. You had your chance with me and you blew it. No, I only want your clothes off so I can be sure our conversation isn't being recorded."

Johnny smiled. "Paranoid much?"

Nora shrugged. "Last I knew, a cop was headed to your house. I thought you would be in jail by now, but here you are in my house instead. It does strike me as curious." She twirled a finger in the air. "Off with it all, Johnny. Every last thread. Why are you dressed like that anyway?"

He tugged off the ball cap and dropped it on the glass coffee table. "Like what?"

"Like a burglar."

She was referring to his all-black attire. In addition to the black jeans and ball cap, he was wearing a plain black T-shirt. The outfit couldn't be more removed from the colorful garb he would normally wear, which was the whole point.

He stood up and pulled the shirt over his head. "I drove out to the country to bury what was left of Lily. I buried her deep, but there's always a chance she could be discovered. I didn't want to be recognizable to anyone who might have spotted me in the vicinity."

"Sound thinking."

Johnny stepped out of his shoes and unbuttoned the jeans. Despite what she'd said, there was a lascivious twist to Nora's mouth as she watched him slide the zipper down. Her eyes sparkled with amusement as he stepped out of his jeans.

Nora gestured with her finger again. "Undies, too."

"Can't you already tell I'm not wearing a wire?"

She rose smoothly from the sofa and slid a hand inside his boxers, making him gasp as her soft hand first cupped his balls then slid along the length of his cock. Her other hand entered his boxers from behind and probed at his ass. The inspection went on far longer than technically necessary to determine the absence of a wire. She smiled and pressed herself against him as he grew hard in her hand.

Her voice became husky. "Perhaps I spoke too soon. Maybe I'll take you for one last spin after we've talked our shit out."

Johnny shuddered as Nora released his hard-on. She reclaimed her place on the sofa and smirked up at him. Feeling ridiculous just standing there with his dick tenting the front of the boxers, Johnny hurriedly pulled his clothes on and sat back down.

He took a bigger sip from the bottle of Stella. "All right, so that's settled. Now tell me about Barry."

Nora shrugged. "Yes, he helped me. Of course he did. He did all the dirty work. Mostly all I did was stand around and give orders, though I did help him with carrying things when necessary."

"The bookcase."

Nora nodded. "The bookcase. And Lily."

Johnny's expression darkened. "About Lily…"

"The easiest part of the whole deal, actually. I drove back by later and saw you were gone. The whore's car was still there, though, so I decided to check on things." There was a disdainful cast to her features as she shook her head. "Thanks for not locking the door, by the way. Made it simple to just walk in and kill her. I used your precious ball bat to bash her worthless fucking brains in."

"No."

"Yes."

Johnny scowled. "Goddammit. I loved that fucking bat. What did you do with it?"

Nora laughed. "You'll never see it again. Grown boys shouldn't have toys, anyway."

Johnny sighed. "All right. So what then?"

"And so then I called Barry. Barry's cousin, Wesley, owns a butcher shop, so that part was easy, too."

"So you hauled Lily's body out to his butcher shop, had him do his thing with her, and then brought her back to my place to, what...fuck with my head?"

Nora nodded. "Sure. Subconsciously, though, I think a part of me still hoped things could work out between us. That's part of what the whole cleanup thing was about. I wanted to save you from yourself after teaching you a lesson. But I got to stewing on things and got madder and madder about the way you treated me. I decided I could do better than you. That I *deserved* better than you."

Johnny grunted humorless laughter and shook his head. "Wow."

Nora smiled. "I'm mercurial, Johnny. Haven't you figured that out yet? I kept changing my mind about you right up to the time I finally left your house this morning."

"But your mind is made up now."

Nora's expression was grim. "It is. There's been no going back since the moment I called Joe Voss, though now I'm thinking an anonymous call to 911 would have worked better. I guess all my hints sailed right over his head. Otherwise you wouldn't still be a free man."

Despite his disgust at the things Nora had told him, Johnny managed a smile. "He did mention your comment about leftovers, but you definitely should have been more explicit than that if you wanted to see me in handcuffs."

"I suppose so." Nora sighed. "I must admit, I expected you to crack under pressure and blab all to your cop buddy."

"Weren't you afraid I'd point the finger at you?"

Nora smiled. "Oh, I counted on it, even sort of looked forward to laughing off your allegations when they interviewed me. I'd covered up everything, so I wasn't worried. And everybody knows the husband or ex is always the culprit in these things. Your accusations would've been laughed off as the delusional rantings of a homicidal maniac. "

Johnny had never imagined Nora would turn on him so completely, or that she was capable of such chilling savagery. Apparently, however, he was just a very bad judge of character, because this made two women in his life who'd committed acts of brutal murder for either no good reason or for reasons vastly insufficient to warrant what they had done.

All while displaying no remorse whatsoever.

It was pretty fucked up.

"What did you promise Barry this time?"

Nora's nose crinkled. "I let them watch while I got naked and molested an embalmed corpse at the funeral home."

Johnny frowned. *"Them?"*

"Barry *and* Wesley." Nora's mouth twisted, her obvious disgust becoming more pronounced. "They were a package deal. There was no way around it. They sat there next to each other with their pants down. Masturbating."

"Jesus."

Nora nodded. "I know. Horrible, right? But totally worth it in the end. Thanks to those giant pervs, I'll never be connected to anything. Also, Barry knows you're here, so if you've got any stupid ideas about revenge, you'd better get them out of your head. In fact, I think it's best if we call the whole thing a wash and forget about it."

"Just move on with our lives. As if nothing ever happened."

She edged a little closer to him, the look on her face more somber now. "The dead are dead, Johnny, and what's done is done. Why waste time sulking over it when you can just get on with things?

She put a hand on his knee.

Johnny got to his feet.

Nora rose with him and clutched at his wrist. "Don't run off, Johnny. Why don't you stay a while?" Her smile was back. "You haven't even finished your beer."

Johnny shook his head. "I learned what I came here to learn. I'm gonna go. But don't worry, doll. Your secrets are safe with me."

She started to protest again.

Johnny reared back and drilled a fist straight into the center of her face.

Nora's nose snapped and gushed blood as she crashed to the floor and wailed in pain. She tried to scramble away from Johnny when he came after her, but he caught up to her and seized the front of her dress. The fabric began to tear as he lifted her off the floor and smashed his fist into her face two more times.

Johnny let go of her and she fell limp to the floor. He stared at her until he was sure she wasn't going anywhere.

Then he went out to the kitchen and opened the door to the deck.

Joe Voss pushed Bree Sloan through the door and into the kitchen. The woman was handcuffed and had a gag in her mouth. Her head wobbled on her shoulders and she moved with the sluggish gracelessness of the drugged. As far as Johnny knew, however, Joe hadn't drugged her. Instead there were multiple welts and gashes on her face, evidence she'd fought like mad. Johnny suspected she might have prevailed if Joe hadn't used his cop status to get the drop on her.

"Where's Lily?"

A gun was clutched in Joe's right hand. He kept it pressed against the back of Bree's head as he glanced at Johnny. "Out on the deck. You bust up the cunt's face like I said?"

Johnny nodded. "See for yourself. She's in the living room. I'll grab Lily."

Out on the deck was a large Igloo cooler. It was red. The color of blood. How fucking appropriate. The cooler contained what was left of Lily. He grabbed the handle on its side and dragged it into the kitchen, wheeling it to a stop in front of Nora's refrigerator. Soon the contents of the refrigerator would be removed and replaced with what was in the cooler.

But that was for later.

They had other business to take care of first.

Johnny joined his friend in the living room. Nora was mewling on the floor and Bree was on the sofa. Joe had his gun aimed at Bree's face. He removed a billy club from a clip attached to his belt and tossed it to Johnny. "Finish her. I want to be out of here in less than ten minutes."

Nora whimpered and tried to crawl away from Johnny as he approached her.

He stopped her with a knee to her chest. He had to work hard to keep his face a tight, emotionless mask as she turned her tear-stained face to look at him. "I didn't want this, Nora. I never wanted anything like this. This is your fault. This is what you've made me. This is what you've forced me into."

Joe made a disgusted sound. "Stop with the speechifying and just do it already."

Johnny did it.

He slammed the club into her head as hard as he could and then did it again, blood flying as her skin split apart. He kept hitting her. Over and over, until there was no doubt she was dead.

Johnny stood up.

Joe tugged a shiny black plastic trash bag from a rear pocket and tossed it on the coffee table. He nodded at Johnny. "In there."

Johnny shook the bag open and dropped the billy club inside.

Joe took a look around at the living room. His gaze settled on the coffee table. "That beer. Yours?"

"Yeah."

"Pour it out, drop it in the bag."

Johnny nodded.

After that, he worked fast, emptying out the refrigerator while Joe stood watch over the semi-conscious woman on the sofa. All the food items first went on the table. He then packed Lily into the fridge. Handling her remains—especially in so callous a way—still made him queasy, but the feeling was nowhere near as intense as it had been the first time he'd seen her cut up like this. A lot had happened since then. He'd become a hypocrite by entering into the same kind of murder pact his so-called morals had caused him to reject just a day ago.

He felt hollow inside.

Empty.

Barely human at all.

But Nora was right, wasn't she?

Dead is dead and what's done is done.

The food items went in the garbage bag. Paper towels soaked up moisture the frozen items left on the table's surface. The paper towels went in the garbage bag, too. The garbage bag went in the cooler.

Johnny rejoined Joe in the living room.

Joe glanced at him. "You park down the street like I told you?"

Johnny put on his black hat. "Yeah."

Joe nodded in approval. His gaze remained locked on Bree Sloan's face. The woman's fuzzy look was dissipating some. She was looking more alert by the second. But Johnny thought he saw resignation in her eyes now, as well as a strange haunted quality. For someone who had fought so hard, she looked like she was ready to die.

Johnny didn't want to watch her die.

He didn't want any of this.

Joe chuckled. "Funny thing. After I beat on her a while, this gal confessed to killing Jamie Benton. Some drunken dispute over money. Jamie had plenty and they didn't. They were all deep in debt to some drug-dealing broads named Dez and Echo. Bree says Lily had nothing to do with it. But Lily was so fucked up she was suggestible. This one and Slick made her think she had done it. Which means…"

Johnny dragged a hand over his face. "Which means Lily never killed anyone and all this was for nothing."

"That's how this shit usually goes, Johnny. People kill each other over stupid shit or for no reason all the time. Be glad you're not a cop, that's all I gotta say." Joe moved closer to the sofa and addressed Bree with a strangely tender tone. "You're a tough chick. I admire that, so I feel like I should tell you what the story's gonna be. You three gals were in a lesbian love triangle. The dead broad on the floor." He jerked his chin in Nora's direction. "She was obsessed with you. She was jealous of the attention you were giving your live-in lover, Lily, so she had her sliced and diced into a bunch of little pieces, the sick fucking bitch. When you found out, you confronted her and the two of you pounded hell out of each other. In fact, you beat on this one so hard, you beat her to fucking death, at which point you became distraught and shot yourself in the face with a legally purchased firearm registered in your name."

Bree made a sound that might have been a muffled laugh.

Joe smiled. "Yeah. Pretty good story, huh? Think my colleagues will buy it?"

Bree lifted her shoulders in a tired shrug.

Joe nodded. "I think they will. Homicide cops in this town ain't the most diligent investigators in the world. And it's not like any of you ladies will be around to tell anyone any different. I'll manufacture a few other little bits of evidence to seal the deal."

He shot Bree in the face.

Johnny grimaced.

Joe spent a few final moments staging the scene. He removed Bree's gag—now blood-soaked—and removed the handcuffs from her wrists. After that, he slid the gun into one of her hands, gingerly curling her dead fingers around its grip.

When it was done, Johnny said, "Barry Miller has a cousin. Wesley. He's involved in this, too."

Joe nodded. "I'll take care of Wesley." He clapped a hand on Johnny's shoulder, jostling him. "It's done, brother."

Johnny frowned. "Are you sure this was the right way to do this? Miller could've burned them all up for us. This just seems so...messy."

"Trust me, you want bodies. Bodies and a story. That means a tidy resolution. There's nothing an investigator loves more. If they just disappeared without a trace never to be heard from again, it'd always be hanging over you. There'd always be questions. There'll be questions anyway, but this way you'll have the answers the homicide guys will want to hear. Let's get the fuck out of here."

Johnny grabbed the cooler on the way out.

It was much lighter than before.

They left the house through the back door.

29

Earlier in the day...

Johnny told him everything.

He cracked under pressure. This despite knowing there was a good chance he could have sent Joe on his way without having divulged anything. Later he wasn't able to say why he wound up spilling his guts. He guessed it was a combination of the rough physical shape he was in and sheer terror fatigue. A big part of him was just bone-weary of being afraid and off-balance. There was no doubt those things had been factors, but Johnny suspected a lot of it was nothing more than unthinking impulse. He'd known Joe most of his life and wasn't accustomed to keeping secrets from him.

So he'd just blurted it out.

Joe said nothing for a long time. He just sat in a rocking chair in Johnny's living room and stared into a middle distance, his expression unreadable. It was like he was in a trance. During that time, Johnny was afraid to say anything. So he followed his friend's lead and just sat there in silence, feeling far calmer than he should.

At last, Joe snapped out of it and rubbed at his eyes. "I'm gonna have a look. Don't go anywhere."

Johnny didn't say anything.

After Joe had taken a long look inside the refrigerator, he returned to the living room and sat again in the rocking chair. Another period of silence ensued, but it wasn't as long. It was at that point that Joe demanded to know all. Johnny complied without hesitation and held nothing back. He started with a detailed account of what he'd seen and heard while hiding out in the closet at Lily's place and concluded nearly a half hour later with Joe's arrival at his door. He hit all the high points in between, including his self-defense killing of Slick and the subsequent disposal of the corpse at the funeral home, as well as the clashes with Lily and her attempts to blackmail him. The only time Joe reacted visibly was when Johnny talked about his drunken drive home and the fight at the convenience store.

"Goddammit, Johnny. Are you ever gonna start listening to me? Never drive hammered. How many times do I have to tell you?"

Johnny was still feeling stiff from his night on the bathroom floor. His face twisted in pain as he shifted uncomfortably on the sofa. "Yeah, yeah, I know. I'm a fuckin' asshole. What else is new? I guess my goose is cooked, huh?"

Joe did some more of that increasingly disturbing staring into space thing. Then his expression turned grave and he said, "I'm gonna help you get out of this, buddy."

Johnny laughed, but there was little actual humor in the sound. "There's no way out of this, Joe." He jerked a thumb in the direction of the kitchen. "You saw that horror movie bullshit in my fridge. There's no undoing that."

Joe nodded. "That's right. There's no undoing it. But what we *can* do is change the narrative."

Johnny frowned. "Huh? Say again?"

"You've been set up. And what is a frame up but a way to create a false impression of events? It's storytelling, Johnny." He smiled. "All we have to do is change the story, fix things to create a different impression of events, the one *we* want people to see. It'll take some work, but if we act fast, I promise you we can make it happen."

Johnny's instinct was to scoff. He felt like Joe was pulling his leg. This had to be a joke. But the look on his friend's face said otherwise. He'd never seen the man look so serious, not even when he was scolding Johnny about driving under the influence.

A tiny flicker of hope ignited in Johnny and set his heart to racing.

"You really think you can do that?"

Joe's nod was emphatic. "Brother, I *know* we can. We're gonna need the cooperation of that assfuck from the funeral home. We'll want him saying the right things when my friends in homicide start looking into this. I'll pay him a visit and convince him helping us is in his best interests."

"How will you do that?"

The barely perceptible smile that touched the corners of Joe's mouth then was more than a little unsettling. "You leave that up to me. Trust me, it won't be a problem. But, Johnny, you're gonna have to get your hands dirty before this is over."

"What do you mean? They're already pretty goddamn dirty."

"I mean this will involve killing some people. Now, don't look at me that way. I know what you're thinking. But you ask me, these are people who deserve to die. They won't be any big loss to society. And changing the narrative alone won't be enough. What you need is a clean slate. A *clean* fucking slate. You understand?"

Johnny nodded.

Joe was talking about killing Nora and anyone else involved. Johnny said nothing at all for a few moments and Joe didn't press him, probably because the other man correctly surmised he'd already made the decision to go ahead with his plan. The decision was made only because he had no other viable way to go. He didn't want to kill Nora. Hell, just yesterday he'd thought she was someone he could fall in love with. A more fucked-up turn of events he could not imagine. It was just fundamentally *wrong* on every level.

But he wanted to go to jail for the rest of his life even less than he wanted to kill Nora.

In the end, that was the deciding factor.

Hell, it was the *only* factor that really mattered.

He looked at Joe. "Why, man? Why are you doing this?"

Joe scowled. "Because you're my brother, man. Maybe not my blood brother, but my brother nonetheless. So don't ask me that question again, because it's fucking insulting."

Johnny wasn't quite ready to let it go. "But you're a cop. Isn't this against everything you stand for?"

Joe laughed. "Brother, I'm not a homicide detective. I'm just a lowly beat cop. All I care about is keeping drunks like you off the road. Anything else, I don't give a shit. Hell, you could run a meth lab up in here, set yourself up as a high-end pimp, what the fuck do I care?"

Johnny gave his old friend a long, squinty-eyed look. Then he shook his head. "Goddamn. You are fucking crazy."

"What? You're just now figuring that out?"

They both laughed.

They discussed things a bit longer and soon Joe suggested Johnny should maybe have a little hair of the dog.

Johnny did not disagree.

30

Three days later…

At five minutes past three in the afternoon, Johnny walked into the Delirium Lounge and claimed his usual seat at the bar. The bar wasn't crowded yet. He'd made it in a little ahead of the after work rush. It was the first time he'd been back since the night Lily died. A Cubs game played soundlessly on the wall-mounted television behind the bar. It was the bottom half of the seventh inning and the Cubs were trailing the Nationals by ten runs. A blowout, or what old-timers like his dad would have called a "laugher."

Riley was behind the bar. She smiled when she saw him. "Wow, the rumors are true. Johnny Doyle is still among the living."

Johnny plucked a cigarillo out of his Hawaiian shirt's breast pocket. "You can't keep a good man down."

"Is that what you are, Johnny? A good man?"

Johnny's expression turned thoughtful as he lit up the cigarillo. He snapped his Zippo shut and dropped it in his breast pocket. "I don't know about that. All I know is I'm not the man I always thought I was."

"That a good thing or a bad thing?"

Johnny sighed. "That's what I've been trying to decide. I'm not sure yet."

Riley leaned against the bar and braced her chin on an upraised palm. "You know what I think?"

Johnny turned his head aside and exhaled smoke. "I do not, but I'm sure you'll tell me."

There was a playful glint in her eye as Riley turned her head first to the left and then to the right, as if checking for prying eyes. She then leaned across the bar and dropped her voice to a whisper. "I think you're hot."

Johnny puffed on his cigarillo. "Is that right?"

"Yep. You know…for an old guy."

Johnny laughed.

Making the male patrons feel special was part of how she earned her living. The smile of a pretty girl like Riley had a way of filling the tip jar fast. And Johnny was notorious for his overly generous tipping. Still, this felt like something a little more than the standard manipulation-through-flirtation routine.

Riley leaned closer and dropped her voice even lower. "You should take me to your place tonight."

She was almost close enough to kiss. He couldn't raise his cigarillo to his mouth without the tip burning her cheek. "How old are you, Riley?"

"Older than you think."

Johnny shook his head. "Not an acceptable answer. How old?"

Riley rolled her eyes. "Twenty-five. There. You happy?"

Johnny shrugged. "I'm just glad you're legal."

"Why? Because you wouldn't want to fuck me otherwise?" Her smirking little smile matched her naughty tone. "Would that make you a *bad* man, Johnny?"

Johnny tapped his cigarillo against the edge of the ashtray. "I reckon it would, Riley. Fortunately that's not an issue."

Riley plucked the cigarillo from his fingers and leaned back a little. She wedged his smoke in a corner of her mouth and puffed on it. "Your place. Tonight. It's settled."

Johnny grunted. "Just like that?"

She nodded, puffed again. "Just like that."

"Okay, then."

Riley laughed.

"Hey, Riley?"

"Yeah, Johnny?"

"Did you know that the cosmic center of the universe is in Murfreesboro?"

She blew a cloud of smoke at him. "Oh, yeah?"

Johnny nodded. "The actual center is inside Davis Market. You know, that little corner grocery where all you collegiate types load up on beer for your parties. They say if you ever set foot in the store, you'll either never leave Murfreesboro or you'll come back after moving away. That's how strong the store's pull is. It's a curse, you see."

Riley studied his expression a moment before replying. "Is this a real thing, Johnny? Or is it just some shit you're making up to fuck with me?"

Johnny put a hand to his chest. "Swear to God."

Riley frowned. "This curse…can it be broken?"

"There's a tree near Peck Hall on the MTSU campus. Legend has it the curse can be broken by nailing a shoe to the tree."

Riley's eyes got big behind her cats-eye glasses and she jabbed the smoldering cigarillo at Johnny. "I've *seen* that tree! Those fucking shoes. I always wondered about that. Holy shit. You're *really* not making any of this up?"

Johnny shook his head. "Nope."

"Change of plans, Johnny. We're visiting that tree tonight. I'm sure I've got a shoe I can spare."

Johnny smiled. "I take it you've set foot inside Davis Market."

"Many fucking times."

Johnny nodded. "And you'd really rather not spend the rest of your life in this town."

Riley laughed. "Damn straight. I mean, I'm not superstitious or anything, but why take chances with that shit? Hey, nothing against the 'Boro, but I'd hate to be locked down to one place forever."

Johnny smiled.

Good.

He liked Riley. She was good people. This thing with her, whatever it was, would be a passing thing. A very short-lived thing, probably. He knew that and was okay with it. It was how it should be. The idea of Riley one day venturing forth into the wider world and having the kind of adventures only the young can have pleased him. Maybe now and then her thoughts would turn to him and perhaps she would think of him fondly when they did.

And maybe not.

He suspected a day would come when she'd forget she'd ever known him.

And that would be okay, too.

Nothing was forever.

The universe had gone out of its way to emphatically make that point lately. He now had a more finely-honed understanding of the limits of mortality than he'd ever wanted.

Johnny frowned.

Another bout of melancholy was looming. It was understandable, given all that had gone down. The last few days had been especially rough, dealing with the cops and their questions. He'd thought they would never be done with him, but then they were, just as Joe had predicted. There was no direct evidence tying him to anything and it was easier all-around for them to accept the narrative Joe had constructed. It hadn't hurt that an array of acquaintances associated with all three women had come forward to share rumors and hearsay, much of it providing circumstantial corroboration of lesbian or bisexual tendencies on the parts of the deceased. It was a weird bit of cosmic synchronicity Johnny chose to interpret as proof he'd done the right thing in going along with Joe's scheme.

Which a part of him knew was bullshit. But people all over the world believed in all kinds of bullshit just so they could sleep at night.

Why should he be any different?

Riley put the cigarillo in the ashtray. "All right, Johnny. The Delirium Lounge is a goddamn bar, right? I know you didn't just come here for my pretty face. So what'll you have? The usual?"

Johnny tapped the bar's surface with a forefinger. "Give me four shots of straight whiskey." He pushed the ashtray aside. "Set 'em up right here."

Riley poured the shots and set them on the bar.

Johnny picked up the first one and stared at the amber liquid inside.

This one's for you, Lily. Part of me's always gonna love you.

The drink went down the hatch. He picked up the second shot.

This one's for you, Nora. For what might have been.

The second shot went down faster and burned a little.

Johnny picked up the third shot.

This one's for you, Bree Sloan. You were tough as nails.

He knocked back the third shot and slammed the empty glass on the bar. He picked up the last shot and felt another twinge of melancholy as he eyed it.

This one's for you, Jamie Benton. I'm sorry you got caught up in this and I'm sorry you got killed.

Riley applauded as he slammed down the last empty glass. "Bravo, Johnny. You deserve some kind of alcoholic achievement badge. What'll you have now?"

Johnny relit the cigarillo with his Zippo. That was a question he didn't have to give much thought. He snapped the Zippo shut and pocketed it.

"Whiskey. Maker's Mark."

Riley reached for the bottle.

Johnny exhaled smoke. "Oh, and make it a double."

THE END

ABOUT THE AUTHOR:

Bryan Smith is the author of numerous previous novels and novellas, including 68 Kill, The Killing Kind, House of Blood, Depraved, The Freakshow, Soultaker, Deathbringer, The Dark Ones, and The Diabolical Conspiracy. Most of these were first available via mass market paperback from Dorchester Publishing. Some have since been reprinted by Deadite Press. All are now available in Kindle editions. A new novel, The Late Night Horror Show, was released by Samhain Publishing in March of 2013. A second novel from Samhain, Go Kill Crazy!, is slated for February 2014. Bryan lives in Tennessee with a wide array of pets. Visit his home on the web at
www.bryansmith.info.

AFTER THE BIO DOUBLE-SECRET BONUS TIDBIT:

Just a little note for anyone reading this far. Johnny's "cosmic center of the universe" anecdote in the final chapter is an actual MTSU campus legend in Murfreesboro, TN, though it's one largely forgotten today. See the link below to see some rotting old shoes nailed to a tree.
http://smg.photobucket.com/user/fearscribe/media/CosmicCenter_zps7da7b2c7.jpg.html

Printed in Great Britain
by Amazon.co.uk, Ltd.,
Marston Gate.